SHE ONCE DISAPPEARED

AN ARTEMIS BLYTHE MYSTERY THRILLER

GEORGIA WAGNER

CONTENTS

1. Chapter 1   1

2. Chapter 2   15

3. Chapter 3   24

4. Chapter 4   32

5. Chapter 5   42

6. Chapter 6   55

7. Chapter 7   62

8. Chapter 8   70

9. Chapter 9   82

10. Chapter 10   93

11. Chapter 11   105

12. Chapter 12   115

13. Chapter 13   123

14.	Chapter 14	133
15.	Chapter 15	150
16.	Chapter 16	165
17.	Chapter 17	175
18.	Chapter 18	191
19.	Chapter 19	199
20.	Chapter 20	205
21.	Chapter 21	218
22.	Chapter 22	233
23.	Chapter 23	246
24.	Chapter 24	255
25.	Chapter 25	264
26.	What's Next for Artemis	276
27.	Also by Georgia Wagner	278
28.	Want to know more?	280
29.	About the Author	282

CHAPTER 1

Artemis Blythe stood drenched and terrified, water tapping around her, as she stared at the glaring headlights of the sedan.

Otto Blythe, the Ghost-killer, emerged from the back seat of the warden's car, a free man. He stood under the rain-soaked skies, a smile twisting his cheeks.

Otto had neat, silver hair that dangled in curls daintily around his ears. He gently massaged his wrists as the warden uncuffed him and sent him striding with his ever-confident gait toward his daughter.

He had the energy of a man half his age and smiled warmly as he drew near, his whole face lighting up with the expression, even as raindrops streaked his features.

"Artemis, dear!" he called out, beaming. "I *knew* you'd come around."

Her father closed the gap between them, but she held out a hand, snapping, "Wait! Stop!"

He froze. Five paces away, watching her quizzically as if he couldn't fathom why on earth she might want him to hang back.

The warden's car door slammed. Doler's phone was out the window, recording a video of the two of them. Further insurance, she supposed. But he wouldn't need it.

The warden's car screeched as it rushed past them, spraying mud against both of their pant legs.

And then it disappeared, angry brake lights vanishing behind the trees, leaving the father and daughter alone in the dark, in the forest preserve parking lot, without a witness in sight.

Artemis Blythe's heart pounded, and it felt as if she were trapped in a dream.

She stared at the Ghost-killer, and he smiled back at her.

As she faced the monster from her past, the man whose actions had stolen *everything* from her, it almost felt as if she were having an out-of-body experience.

Her heart pounded, and it was as if she could hear the blood rushing in her ears. She stared at her father, eyes narrowed, breathing in shallow puffs. Her fingers tapped against the hem of her sweater, which was damp like her hair and skin.

She didn't know what she was supposed to say.

That was the strangest part.

All of this effort, all of this sacrifice—she'd found the truth about a decades old case in order to blackmail the warden of her father's prison.

She'd left Cameron Forester behind—gunshots resounding in the house they'd been hiding in. She still didn't know if he'd been shot.

A lance of worry jolted through her.

But Otto Blythe was now leaning in, arms extended as if to hug her.

And so, she kneed him in the groin.

It was an instinctual thing, really. One moment his arms spread, attempting to wrap around her, the next her knee arching up and slamming between his unmentionables.

He made a sound like a leaking balloon, doubling over and gasping at the ground. Water poured from his lips, and he rasped at the mud, wheezing.

Artemis stepped hurriedly back from him, not even daring to shove him—she didn't want to *touch* the man.

"Don't come near me!" she snarled.

He was gasping, groaning at the ground. When he looked up, his damp silver curls flicked water and he breathed heavily a few times, mouth forming a small circle. He was still half bent, hands resting on his knees now as the ex-mentalist glared at her.

"What the hell, Art?" he said once he'd recovered his breath, in a chiding tone like a doting father disappointed with his grade-school child.

"Don't call me that," Artemis snapped, pointing a finger at him. For a brief moment, she wondered what she might do if she had a gun. "Don't!"

He tried to rise now, slowly, hands spread as if in surrender. He stepped gingerly back, keeping well-clear of any more errant knees. He shot a look over his shoulder in the direction where the warden's car had vanished and then looked back at her. "We shouldn't stay here, dear," he said. "That Doler fellow did *not* seem very happy with you. Some of the things he said. Tut, tut—someone should wash his mouth out with soap."

"Shut up," Artemis snapped. And her words were like the verbal version of what her knee had just done.

He stared at her, blinking. "I'm . . . I'm confused," he said, wincing a final time, but placing his hands on his hips now. "*You* rescued me from that prison."

"Rescued?" she snorted. "I broke you out of jail where you were serving a sentence for multiple homicide."

Her father shrugged. "Yes, but . . . but of course you know I'm innocent," he said simply. He frowned, peering at her, blinking water droplets from his eyes and looking like some scorned puppy left on the side of the road. "You *know* that now, don't you? Why else would you

4

rescue me?" He stared at her, his expression quizzical, his head tilting to the side.

He had a way of organizing his features, his motions so that he looked so very innocent. But she knew what he'd done.

Her father was the Ghost-killer because—save that one error in fore-sight with the dead woman in his bed—most of his crimes had been committed without leaving a trace, in locked homes, strangling his victims slowly to leave as little damage as possible. Just like an invisible man.

At least seven young women, possibly more.

All of them had *looked* or *behaved* like Helen Blythe in some way. This was why Artemis had first assumed her father had killed Helen as well. . . Killing young women who reminded him of his own daughter before finally turning on the source of his angst. Her father's victims had all been intelligent, beautiful, and even had Helen's curled, auburn hair.

And so, for a time, Artemis had assumed her sister dead.

But now . . . she hoped Helen was still alive.

Too many moving pieces.

She couldn't keep track of it all. Fake-Helen's claims over the phone. . . Tommy's claims about meeting their sister at a waterfall, being handed a note.

What was Artemis supposed to *believe*?

5

Now, she scowled at where her father looked at her with an earnest expression.

"Artemis," he said, his voice pleading, like the bleating of a sheep. But his eyes were those of a wolf. "Please, listen to me. . ." He reached out a trembling hand as if to grip her arm.

She raised a threatening finger.

He winced, didn't touch her, but kept his hand extended, the fingers trembling, water droplets tumbling from where his palm shook. "I never killed a soul," he whispered, his eyes still fixated on her. "And now that I'm out . . . *finally,* I can clear my name." He swallowed, then blew droplets of water from his lips, still standing under the tapping rain. "Will you help me?"

She was still inhaling shakily, still breathing slowly. Artemis didn't believe him, of course. Her own father had threatened her the last time she'd visited. He'd arranged to have hallucinogens brought *into* the prison and blackmailed people with it.

He'd been visited by Mr. Kramer—Jamie's father—before Kramer had killed his own wife. It was all a ruse. . .

And she was growing so very tired of it.

She said, quietly, "Either you get in the car, keep your mouth shut, and come with me. Or. . ." She shrugged, waving a hand off into the woods. "See how long you can last on foot. You know where we are, don't you? This preserve is fifty miles from civilization."

It was closer to forty . . . but fifty had a better ring to it. Besides, she'd chosen this particular drop-off point with the warden for a reason.

She needed her father to feel alone, isolated. Needed him to come with her.

And then. . .

Then she'd place the call.

A phone call she'd been dreading for days now.

Her hand lingered near her pocket, feeling the rigid, rectangular outline of her cellular device through her damp trousers. And then she shrugged and turned, walking back up the wet asphalt toward where she'd asked Tommy to leave the getaway vehicle.

She peered through the woods, hesitant, but then spotting the green tarp amidst the northern copse of trees facing the mountains on the horizon.

She moved toward the vehicle, a skip to her step, hastening forward. She grabbed at the tarp, the water slick under her fingers, but then glanced back, peering toward where her father remained standing in the parking lot, wearing a frown.

He watched her, hesitant, and then let out a faint, leaking sigh.

He began to move toward her, hands in his pockets, head hung low, his silver curls encumbered with drops of rainwater. She stood under the trees now, momentarily protected from the deluge, frowning in the direction of the Ghost-killer.

Innocent.

What a marvelous claim. She hadn't believed him the first time. Or the twenty other times he'd said it. Her father was a murderer. He'd killed seven women and the evidence had been ironclad. She'd seen it all herself.

So what had changed?

Her feet shuffled, kicking pine needles and scraping through detritus. She let out a shaking little sigh, frowning again.

Perhaps . . . perhaps her *own* experience had changed her mind.

The feds, *everyone* had been convinced Artemis had murdered Azin, the chess master. The video surveillance had proved it. The blood on her sweater. . .

All of it.

And yet it hadn't been true.

She'd been framed.

Her father was still moving toward her, slowly, glancing about as if catching his bearings. He paused to pick up a small pinecone, tossing it a couple of times, rolling it in his hand and then placing it primly in his pocket.

She wondered what it was like to breathe free air for the first time in a decade and a half.

She felt a jolt in her chest.

Her father's smiling eyes found her, the creases along his face now more furrowed, deeper than she remembered. His silver curls plastered to his face, his intelligent eyes watching her, cautious.

She didn't *want* to feel a rising tide of sympathy. She didn't want to feel *anything* toward her father. She'd come here on a mission.

Jamie was in danger. Sophie was in danger.

She only had a couple of days left to deliver the Ghost-killer to the kidnapper. That had been the deal. Jamie and Sophie and an alibi for Azin's murder in exchange for Otto Blythe.

A simple trade.

Artemis had come this far, hadn't she?

Only a phone call now.

Where do you want to meet?

A simple call.

And yet. . .

Her father reached the forest fringe, still watching her, curious and attentive. He was playing with her emotions even now. She could feel it in the slump of his shoulders, the slack, gentle expression he carried in every crease and crevice of his features.

This man didn't belong on the other side of a locked door, and yet here he stood, free as a bird.

And her heart pounded as he approached.

"I know you did it," she said quietly, watching as he drew near. "I've seen the evidence."

He took another step toward her, and the green tarp left in the copse. He glanced at the tarp, then back at her. He waved a hand like a conductor's wand at the tarp. "Tommy?" he asked, raising an eyebrow.

She nodded once.

He smiled and took another step.

"I always could count on Tommy," the Ghost-killer said.

"Your fingerprints were found on three of the victims," she snapped.

"Planted," he replied, shrugging.

"The murder weapon—a cord of rope—was found beneath the floorboards under your bed."

He looked at her pensively. "You know me, Art ... er, Artemis. Do you think I'd be stupid enough to *keep* a murder weapon?"

"I didn't know you'd be stupid enough to kill seven young women," Artemis shot back.

He shrugged.

"The body found in your bed. The last victim. It was seen on *camera*," she replied.

He watched her. "Also planted. Someone wanted me to take the fall, Art. Someone wanted me in trouble."

"Who?" she snapped.

"The same person who took your sister!" he replied, his eyes narrowed. And for the first time in a long while, his voice shook with something on the verge of a genuine emotion. "I miss her too," he murmured. "I've done what I could behind bars . . . but now." He exhaled deeply, adjusting his wrists and leaning back. "*Now* I can find her. A father should never have been prohibited from finding out what happened to his firstborn child."

Artemis stared at him, and then a smile split her face. She chuckled softly, shaking her head side to side.

"What?" he said, staring at her. "What is it?"

"You almost had me," she said. "For a second there. . . I almost thought. . ." She trailed off, shaking her head and releasing a sigh.

"Artemis," her father said quietly. "I hope you know. . . I am very sorry. For everything." For a moment, his voice seemed to shake again.

But that had always been the problem. She'd never known *when* to take him seriously. He was a chameleon and had always been able to camouflage his true intentions.

She reached for the tarp now, keeping an eye on her father, making sure he stayed back. He wasn't a physically intimidating man. She wasn't concerned about him attacking her. No—he *needed* her. A man recently escaped from prison would soon be wanted by the police. *Everyone* would be looking for him.

He needed her. . .

Besides, she'd suspected that Otto had been the one to hire Fake-Helen. Otto was always behind it, even when she couldn't quite see *how*.

"Really. . . I am very, very sorry," her father was saying, but his voice was somewhat lost in the downpour.

At first, she ignored him. He still stood off to the side, ten paces away. A safe distance.

And that's when she heard the crunching footsteps.

She frowned, turning sharply.

And two figures emerged from behind the nearest and largest tree, coming at her. Both men wore black masks. Both had guns in their hands, and both were moving *fast*.

Sorry. . .

He wasn't apologizing for past sins. But new ones.

A shout burst from her lips, and she stumbled back, but the two masked men kept coming.

One reached out, grabbing her by the arm as she tried to shout. Another had a hood clutched in a gloved hand.

She tried to yank her arm, to kick, but the men moved quickly as if they'd performed this routine before.

A hood was pulled tightly over her face. Her feet scrambled against the ground, but her arm went taut as she was yanked toward the men. Her shout was caught in her lungs. A hood was pulled tight, her arm was gripped in a vice, and then she was shoved forward.

"Shut up and move!" snapped the nearest man.

A voice she didn't recognize.

Her father was protesting now. "Is that really necessary?" he was saying.

And by the sound of things, they were man-handling *him* too.

Not cops. They didn't move like cops.

She was sent stumbling forward by rough hands. Her breath came in rapid gasps, and she was pushed again. She hit the ground, knees gouging into the earth. She was protesting, her voice muffled by the dark hood. Completely blind.

Her father was shouting now too.

But their cries fell on deaf ears, and the two armed men dragged Artemis onto the tarmac. Away from the woods. The soft sensation of cushioned seats. The sound of a slamming door. Then a revving engine.

Muscled arms and shoulders jostled in next to her, pinning her in what felt like a back seat of a large car.

"Don't move," snapped a gruff voice in her ear. "Keep quiet, and we'll be there soon."

Artemis was hyperventilating now. Panic rising within her. The only question seemed *where* was *there*? Who were these men? She hadn't had a chance to call Fake-Helen.

This realization sent terror through her.

Only a couple of days until her deadline was up. Jamie and Sophie would be killed.

And now. . . Otto and Artemis were jammed in some back seat, between two armed men, as a car picked up pace, the engine growling, carrying them hastily away to some unknown location.

CHAPTER 2

They were prodded forward in the dead of night. Artemis' arm scraped against rough, rusted metal. The cold tinge of the jagged edge sent tingles along her arm. She shifted uncomfortably as they moved down some path, leading away from where they'd parked their vehicle.

She exhaled in shallow puffs, shifting uncomfortably with each step forward. The blindfold still concealed her vision, and her heart hammered rapidly.

"Keep moving!" snapped one of the gruff voices of the mask-wearing, gun-toting men.

She continued stumbling on, her mind spinning. Had Fake-Helen sent these goons? How? The kidnapper wouldn't have *known* where Artemis was meeting the warden.

No. . . This was someone else.

She could hear her father breathing in quick gasps next to her, trying to navigate the trail at her side. He also bumped against her, and where his elbow brushed—at least, she assumed it was his elbow—shivers crept along her arm.

She inhaled the scent of mildew and old refuse. But as she brushed against another metal protrusion, images of rusted cars and old metal springs came to mind. Suddenly, she stiffened, breathing slowly.

And then, with a snarl, she ripped the blindfold off.

One of the thugs shouted, leaning in to grab her, but Artemis flung the blindfold at him, yelling, "Tommy! Show yourself, where are you? Really? You sent guys to *kidnap* me?"

The thug's hand had latched onto her arm again, but she yanked away. Now that she'd called her brother's name, the henchman looked sheepish. He was no longer wearing the face mask, displaying dark features with narrowed eyes. The other man, at his side, was taller and wider with a bit of a paunch. This second man had a hooked nose and a potbelly. His facial hair was immaculately trimmed, though, and oiled.

The two men had been escorting Otto and Artemis through a junk-yard.

All around them, towers of rusted metal and old, abandoned items lined the paths. To Artemis' right, she spotted a row of crushed cars, sans windows, stacked on pallets. Off ahead, she spotted a toppled train car, resting on old, torn up train tracks, the metal twisted in spirals.

She exhaled shakily, shooting warning glances at the gunmen, but now stepping forward. Ahead of them toward the train car.

"God dammit, Tommy!" she screamed. "Show your stupid ass!"

Artemis was simply *not* in the mood to be trifled with. She rested her hands on her hips now, glaring ahead.

Her father was muttering behind her, and she noticed him slowly remove his own blindfold, blinking owlishly and running a hand through his silver curls as he stared toward the train car as well.

Artemis had been in this particular junkyard before.

At the time, she'd been fleeing hitmen in hot pursuit of her brother.

Tommy Blythe wasn't much like his sister—Tommy had long been involved with the Seattle mob. And now, she watched as a lanky man with long hair pulled himself up a metal ladder, emerging from the toppled train engine and peering at his two family members from behind a set of designer sunglasses.

The wiry man pulled himself on top of the train engine and then flung his legs over the side, dangling them there. Thin, scrawny some might say, Tommy didn't cut a particularly imposing figure. He raised his sunglasses for a moment, studying her.

She met a familiar gaze. Mismatched eyes—one the hue of wheat fields, the other of glacial rivers. His eye colors were opposite to hers, just like so many other things in contrast between the twins. Tattoos were visible along the edges of his black jacket sleeves.

Two words etched in black ink along his neck, under his chin, and reaching to his ears. They were in a language she didn't understand, and the ink was fading somewhat, but she knew, now, those words were the names of his sisters.

Helen. Artemis.

He'd had their names tattooed on his face.

A single teardrop tattoo also dripped from the corner of his left eye.

He watched her curiously, his legs still dangling in constant motion beneath him. He gave a little wave, his expression impassive. He didn't smile in greeting—he never smiled.

And Artemis returned the dour expression.

She stood in the dust, framed by walls of metal, facing the toppled train engine, and demanded, "What the actual hell, Tommy?"

He winced, glancing from her to Otto. "Sorry, sis," he said, speaking in curt sentences. Tommy was a firm believer in the economy of words. "My bad. Just had to see him."

Tommy was once again glancing at Otto.

Artemis was shaking her head, though, snapping her fingers at the nearest thug. "Give me my phone back!" she demanded. "Now!"

The thug with the beer belly and oiled goatee glanced at Tommy. The long-haired mobster nodded once, his sunglasses flashing in the sunlight.

The mobster sighed, fished a phone from his pocket, and handed it to Artemis.

She snatched it greedily, glancing down and cycling through the numbers.

"Hang on, sis," Tommy said. "Just chill, 'kay?"

She looked up, gripping her phone in a trembling hand. She shook her head adamantly. "No—*you chill*!" she snapped. "Jamie's your friend, too, dammit."

Tommy nodded. "Yeah. . ." he scratched at his chin. "I know. But you got a couple days, don't you?"

She snorted. "What? *No*. Things keep coming up, if you hadn't noticed," she said sarcastically, waving her hands toward the henchmen. "Wasn't expecting a routine kidnapping either. We gotta do it, Tommy. The deal was plain!"

"What deal?" Otto said conversationally. He smiled warmly at Tommy. "Good to see you again, Tomboy!" he called out.

Tommy wrinkled his nose.

"What deal?" Otto insisted, glancing at Artemis.

Tommy slid off the edge of the train, landing on the ground and dusting himself off. He glanced at their father and said, without answering the man's question, "Huh. So you're still an asshole, then?"

Otto blinked. He reached up, brushing his curls aside again. "Pardon me?"

"That's all you got? Fifteen years gone. Good to see you, Tomboy?" Tommy snorted, marching forward now, both of his fists clenched at his side.

Otto winced. "I said it was *good* to see you."

"Yeah, yeah, whatever old man." Tommy shook his head, pointing a long finger at their father. "You know. . . I honestly oughta just let her go through with it."

Otto glanced at Artemis, then back at his son. "Go through with . . . what?"

Artemis was frowning. Tommy was scowling. And Otto's expression had finally moved from politely indifferent to concerned.

But their father had always been a master of controlling his facial expression. A manipulator through and through, he kept his features polite but mildly puzzled.

Still, he didn't blink.

Focused, enraptured by what Tommy had been saying.

Worried.

But he didn't need to be. He'd been the one to orchestrate all of this, hadn't he?

"Dammit, Tom," Artemis said. "You were just supposed to leave a vehicle. Not get yourself involved. So what is this, huh? Wanna beat dad up a bit before he goes bye-bye?"

Tommy shook his head. "Thought about it." The man had come to a halt five paces away now, feet at shoulder width, shoulders thrown back, eyes narrowed into cold slits. "But something came up."

"What's going on?" Otto insisted.

"Oh, be quiet," Artemis snapped. "You wanted this. Your kidnapping psycho friend did her job. Good for you. All I care about is getting Jamie back."

"Jamie . . . Kramer?" Otto said, excited. "You know, his father visited me in prison."

"We know," Artemis snapped. "And you coached him in how to mur-der his wife!"

"That's . . . not what happened."

"Just be quiet."

Artemis was pacing back and forth, shaking her head and muttering to herself. She knew she couldn't let Otto go free. She just needed him to *think* he was free. Needed him alive to make the swap for Jamie and Sophie. To get the alibi for Azin's murder.

21

CHAPTER 3

Her father was still doubled over, breathing heavily at the ground, hands pressed to his gut. But he looked up slowly, eyes narrowing. "What. . ." he swallowed, then tried again. "What did you say?"

He winced as he massaged his solar plexus, taking a step away from the thug who'd thrown the haymaker.

But Artemis shook her head, her eyes narrowed in scorn. "No," she snapped. "I know what you did. Don't play. Hell, I don't even know why I'm speaking to you. Tommy!" She turned back to her brother, her own off-colored eyes meeting his. "Let us go. Or help me deliver him to his psychotic bitch-friend."

"Hang on!" Otto snapped. His voice cracked like a whip, and when Artemis and Tommy glanced over, they both frowned.

Their father was staring at the two of them, breathing slowly, his nostrils flaring. The junkyard hadn't been subjected to the drizzle at the foot of the mountains, though the skies above were still gray. The scent of rain was coming closer, mingling with the rust and refuse surrounding them.

But something in Otto's voice gave Artemis pause.

She felt shivers up her spine, and pulled absentmindedly at her sleeves, shifting side to side. She was grateful she wasn't still wearing the dress she'd donned for the con with the warden's wife.

Having changed in the car, while Forester had looked away—or at least, claimed he had—she was once again in her preferred ensemble. Sweatpants and a dark sweatshirt. Nothing formfitting. Nothing eye-catching. She didn't wear makeup, and most of her clothing was purchased online. She always ordered a size or two larger than she needed, so there was no point in worrying if the clothing item fit or not.

Artemis had spent a decent amount of time in tournaments or online streaming—in the chess community, many of the fans could abide a smart woman. *Or* a pretty woman.

But both in one?

It wasn't just some men who gave someone like that a hard time. But some kinds of women would happily attempt to destroy the reputation of anyone they were envious of.

Artemis had found herself the target of anyone with an axe to grind.

She'd kept her head low and used soap instead of perfume. Now, most of the scent was that of damp clothing. But standing there, briefly wondering where Forester was—and recalling the gunshots she'd heard when fleeing the house where they'd been cornered—she stared at the expression on her father's face and found that she spotted something that had rarely ever been displayed.

In the widening of his eyes. The flare of his nostrils. The sheer fact that a curl of silver had been left uncombed and out of place instead of hastily brushed back into alignment.

Her father was staring at her with a look of absolute fear.

"Don't," she said, pointing at him. "Don't even start."

"No . . . no, Artemis, *please*," said Otto. He held out both his hands—not the calloused hands of a laborer or fighter. Soft hands. The hands of a thinking man. But now, his voice trembled. "This wasn't your idea?"

"What wasn't?" Tommy cut in.

But Otto was staring at Artemis. "It wasn't your idea to break me out? *Truly*? So . . . so you don't think I'm. . ."

"You're guilty as sin, Dad," Artemis snapped. "What are you even playing at? You think I *wanted* to break you out?"

Her father watched her, breathing in shallow puffs. Then, he whispered, "Oh no. . . No, no . . . no, no, no. . ."

26

He sounded like a radio track caught on repeat. He was shaking his head now, starting to stumble back. And then he began glancing around, wide-eyed, breathing in rapid puffs. "Where!" he was saying. "Where is she? It's her . . . isn't it? No, no, no!"

Tommy nodded at one of his thugs, and the man with the paunch stepped in, snagging Otto's arm, holding him in place.

But Otto tried to yank away, still slipping on the dusty ground. In the distance, thunder rumbled. No flash of lightning—it was hidden behind the clouds, Artemis realized.

"I don't understand," Tommy said quietly. "What's got you spooked, old man?"

But their father was still stumbling, shaking his head, trying to yank his arm free. The panic in his eyes was obvious. And Artemis was nearly roped in by the display. . .

Normally, she wouldn't have cared.

She'd long since given up on trying to believe anything her father said. A lifetime of lies, thousands of lies, and one eventually becomes jaded. The boy who cried wolf had grown up into a man in her father, and he was the least trustworthy person she'd ever met.

But now . . . she frowned, breathing slowly and feeling the way her breath tickled her lips on exit as she released a slow gust of air.

Tommy had a hand out, still playing it cool, and still wearing those sunglasses, despite the overcast skies. Now, Tommy was glancing at their father. "You're saying you didn't hire this kidnapper?" Tommy said lazily.

Otto shook his head, grim, his lips pressed in a thin line now. "No! Never! You have to believe me!"

"I don't. Artemis doesn't, either."

This felt oddly supportive from her brother, and she shot him a quick look of gratitude. Now, the two thugs were closer to Otto, both corralling him so he couldn't turn tail and run. But the Ghost-killer had frozen in place, motionless, hyperventilating and shaking his head.

His hand massaged at his stomach, lingering there.

Briefly, Artemis wondered if her old man suffered from the same panic attacks she sometimes succumbed to. For some reason, the thought sent shivers up her spine. Sharing DNA was bad enough. . . She didn't want to know of any other similarities.

"I didn't hire anyone!" the Ghost-killer snapped.

"So how do you explain this?" Tommy asked, waving a hand and indicating his father's full person.

Otto scowled. "I don't know. This wasn't *my* doing! I thought my children had finally come through—had finally seen the light! Seen my innocence!"

"It doesn't matter how many times you say it," Artemis shot back. "We know you're lying."

But even as she said it, she felt a crack in the facade. A hesitation, a tremor to her voice. She shifted uncomfortably now, rubbing at one hand with a thumb and wincing where she stood. Tommy shot her a quick look, having perhaps picked up on the hesitation in her voice.

Both of them ping-ponged the expression back and forth. Tommy's eyebrow had inched up over his black frames.

Artemis wished she could tell her own subconscious to calm down. Of course her father was lying. Of course he wasn't innocent. She'd seen the evidence. Seen *footage* of the body in his bed with him. His last victim.

He'd killed Abraham Dawkins' first wife—the sheriff's younger spouse. He'd targeted girls that reminded him of Helen.

It had all fit.

It had all made sense.

But two pieces had changed now.

Helen was alive. Tommy had seen her by the waterfall, had been given chess annotation as a message. A secret note.

But also. . .

Artemis had been framed for murder, and this hellish experience had granted her a change in perspective.

She now watched her father with a perspective and an old, familiar frown. He was still shaking his head fervently, holding his hands out, fingers splayed in some silent protest.

Finally, she said, "If you didn't hire her, who did? What does she want with you?"

"Who is it?" her father demanded. "What did she call herself?"

Artemis hesitated, winced. She hadn't mentioned this part to Tommy. "She claimed to be Helen," Artemis said quietly, shrugging once. "She knew details about my childhood. Details only *you* could have provided. But she also *didn't* know things only Helen would have. She didn't know about the letter our sister gave you," Artemis added, glancing at Tommy.

Tommy was staring at her, jaw unhinged. He blinked a few times and then swallowed before resuming his cool, calm, and collected persona. "What the hell? Helen called you?"

"Not Helen," Artemis shot back. "She said she never gave you a letter by the waterfall. She didn't remember it."

"What letter?" Otto snapped, still with terror in his voice.

But Artemis was watching Tommy now, who said, "I saw her." He insisted, "I remember it as clear as day. It was Helen, and I saw her. She gave it to me."

"I believe you," Artemis replied. "The woman on the phone didn't know about it. There were other things she slipped on also. She did

30

her research, but not enough. And who *else* could've helped her research and who *also* wanted the Ghost-killer released from prison?" She turned her accusing gaze to her father now.

The two thugs flanking him were glancing back and forth, eyes darting to and fro as if watching some fascinating sports spectacle.

Artemis hesitated, then shrugged. "You know what—let's find out, shall we?"

She raised her phone.

She'd been tasked with freeing Otto. She'd completed her mission. The priority was to save Jamie and Sophie.

Nothing else even came close.

Conjecture, claims, her father's mind games—it all took a back seat.

She exhaled slowly now, like a woman having snared a life raft, holding on for dear life. So many moving pieces—but one thing was solid.

Jamie.

And so, she raised her phone the thug had returned, glancing significantly at her family members, and dialed the number for Fake-Helen.

31

CHAPTER 4

Artemis' hand shook faintly as she held the phone in front of her face, speaker on.

The dial tone interrupted the silence, and all eyes fixated on the small device. Otto stood to the side, a hand lingering on his midsection, his piercing gaze fixated on his daughter. Tommy was scowling, the expression visible even behind those sunglasses. His arms crossed, his leather jacket creasing as he watched, waiting attentively. The news that Helen had called Artemis clearly had taken him by surprise.

Tommy's two henchmen still lingered back, one of them reclining against a crushed jalopy, the other glancing at the darkening sky above the junkyard.

Thunder rumbled once more, and clouds rolled in like celestial waves, the cottony white carried by a rising breeze.

The phone continued to ring.

And ring.

And—

"Holy shit, you actually did it. High hells—what a rush, huh?" The words exploded the speakerphone, eager and prattling.

Artemis fidgeted uncomfortably, her sweater no longer quite *damp* but not dry yet either, having settled for an uncomfortable middle ground between the two.

The familiar voice sent shivers down her back. An airy, lilting voice. A voice like that of a thespian, a stage actress. Over-the-top, but intentionally so.

A very self-aware voice. A voice aware enough of itself to be entirely indifferent to anyone else's opinion of it.

And now, Artemis could feel shivers along her arms. She swallowed faintly.

The voice was still prattling. ". . . heard about it on the news. Ghost-killer break out. No clues. Guards suspected. Like—*wow*, Artemis. You did it! I knew you could, sis. Er . . . hello? You gonna say anything?"

Another long pause.

For one wild moment, Artemis almost felt like hanging up.

But then, shooting a glance toward her brother and father, standing on that dusty road in the heart of her brother's junkyard, she said,

33

"Hello?" Her voice rasped, and so she swallowed and tried again. "Can you hear me?"

"Yes, Artemis. I can hear you, dear." A chuckle, which was disrupted by static from a bad signal, but then the laughter returned. "Oh this *is* fun. So where is he? Do you have him?"

"Yes," Artemis said quietly. "I . . . I do." She shot a look toward her father, who was staring at the phone with eyes wide.

Tommy took a step closer, leaning in now, studying the phone.

"Well," said the woman, "where can we meet?"

Artemis shook her head. "Hang on . . . I need to know Jamie's alright."

"He is. So is Sophie. Now stop stalling—really. I'm not in the mood, Artemis." The voice on the other end had a jagged edge all of a sudden. And Artemis felt a chill along her back. "I've been waiting a long time for this," said the voice, speaking with the same edge. "And I can't *tell* you how excited I am to meet him. . . After all these years."

Artemis frowned at the phone. "He's the one who hired you, isn't he?"

"Hired? What? No, no. . . This is for my own delight."

Artemis shot a look toward Otto, who was swallowing now, his Adam's apple bobbing with the motion. He was shaking his head from side to side, hurriedly, and still attempting to lean back, as if he could press through the old, rusted refrigerator at his spine.

Artemis frowned. "For your own. . ." she trailed off.

34

"Can he hear me?" said the voice quietly. "Is he there?"

Artemis just stared at the phone, shivering and shaking. "If he didn't hire you, who did?" she demanded.

"I thought I told you. . . No one hired me. I was asked—quite nicely—by a dear friend of mine."

"What friend?" Artemis snapped. "What *friend*?"

This was not how she'd wanted the conversation to go. If her father hadn't been behind his prison break, then who had? The Professor? The old killer who'd claimed to mentor the Ghost-killer?

This Fake-Helen?

But the woman laughed suddenly, and said, "Is that what he's been telling you? The little liar. No, no, no. The friend who asked me to help was the Ghost-killer."

Artemis hesitated. "I . . . that's what I said."

"Is it?" said the woman. "Is it really?"

Artemis stood in the junkyard now, frozen in place, feet at shoulder width and breath coming in shallow puffs. She felt tingles along her spine, and she paused.

"I don't understand."

"No, Art, you really don't, do you?"

"You're implying Otto *isn't* the Ghost-killer," Artemis said.

"Bingo. The Ghost-killer is a friend of mine. Someone I'm . . . *very* close to. Some might even say . . . closer than blood."

Artemis and Tommy both shared a quick look, frowning, then glanced back at the phone.

Otto was still hyperventilating, anxiety written across his features.

Artemis' mind was whirring. Pieces all tangled together. Her father claimed he was innocent. This woman had blackmailed Artemis into freeing Otto from prison.

It was all too confusing.

Who did one trust in a world of liars?

Otto was a liar. Fake-Helen was a liar. They all lied.

So how did she know *who* to believe?

The horrible conclusion was really quite simple: she didn't know.

"Who are you really?" Artemis said at last.

"I told you," the voice said breezily. "I'm bored with that question, Art. Very bored."

"And . . . that note you gave Tommy. Where did that happen again?" Artemis murmured.

"Stop asking me that. I told you—I never gave Tommy any note." The voice had gone irritated now, harsh. After a brief clearing of the throat, though, the woman said, "Enough chatter. Where can we meet?"

Artemis froze, motionless. She'd called, hadn't she? But now that she was faced with the rendezvous, she realized how woefully unprepared she was.

She hesitated, opening her mouth, then closing it again.

She stared toward the men, and they all frowned back at her.

Thankfully, none of them spoke.

Tommy was scowling. Her father still looked frightened.

Artemis said, "Somewhere public. Where we can see each other."

"Alright—what did you have in mind?"

She paused. "I need assurances."

"Honey doll, I can't provide you with any of that. Besides . . . it's gonna take me a few . . . hours to reach you." A chuckle. "I've been on a bit of a spending spree."

Artemis wasn't even sure what this meant. She swallowed, glanced around, then looked back toward her brother.

Tommy was slowly shaking his head. A finger crept up the front of Tommy's chest, crawling over his leather jacket, and then rising toward his sunglasses. A long, extended digit rested against his lips in a shushing gesture.

She frowned at him.

Tommy shook his head more adamantly and pressed the finger to his lips.

Artemis said, "What about outside the hotel in Pinelake?"

"Pinelake, huh? Bold. Sure. I'll be there in five . . . no, no, wait—eight hours, honey. Think you can track that. Eight hours."

"Sure. Yeah . . . yeah, I'll see you in eight."

"One other thing, Art," Fake-Helen began.

But Artemis didn't wait to listen. No more requests. No more blackmail. She'd done what was asked, and she wouldn't do anything further.

Artemis hung up and cursed, staring at Tommy.

"What was that?" Tommy said, slowly.

She didn't reply at first.

It was a bold, risky move. But Fake-Helen was excited. Happy. Artemis was willing to risk that the woman wouldn't lash out. Besides, Artemis was still well within the seven-day window. And standing there, she realized she needed something of a plan. Tommy's goons had gotten the drop on her. There was no telling what Fake-Helen had cooked up for all of them.

Would the woman arrive with thugs of her own?

But now . . . questions were still swirling. She glanced at Tommy.

Immediately, her brother shook his head. "That's not Helen," he said simply.

"I know," Artemis shot back.

"It *could* have been her," Otto retorted, his voice shaking. "It's been years since you've seen your sister."

"You be quiet," Artemis retorted. "I'm still not sure you didn't kill her."

"How could I have?" he exclaimed. "She's on the phone, right now!"

"That's not Helen!" Tommy and Artemis snapped at the same time. The two of them were now facing their father. Both of them breathing heavily, chests rising and falling, arms at their sides, fingers spread.

Artemis' own thoughts went to something else Fake-Helen had said over the phone. The first time they'd interacted, the kidnapper had said, *"You know. . . I always did hate you, Artemis. Always. You were so . . . innocent. Naive. You thought you were so clever. Helen thought you were the star and the moons!"*

Artemis knew this wasn't her sister. Helen had always been Artemis' best friend. Kind, gentle, caring, tenderhearted. The woman on the phone was vain, twisted, and cruel. She enjoyed harming others. And the final line. . . *Helen thought you were the star and the moons!* A note of jealousy. And also referring to Helen as someone *else*. A slip. The kidnapper's anger had made her slip, and so Artemis knew this *wasn't* Helen. It couldn't be.

Helen might have known this woman. Might even have been . . . God forbid . . . *killed* by this woman. But this was not Artemis' sister.

And as she thought it, a slow burning confidence returned to Artemis' chest. A knowledge as deep as marrow. This wasn't her sister.

The thought resounded. It brought hope, brought glimmers of light in a dark night.

Tommy was scowling deeply, but as he did, he reached a hand into his leather jacket, pulling something from his pocket. He lifted it, extending the item toward Artemis, and murmuring as he did so. "She's wrong about the note," he said. "Helen *did* give something to me. I know it was Helen, so whoever this is . . . they weren't there at the time."

"But did you hear her?" Otto was saying excitedly. "The Ghost-killer put her up to it. He's jealous! He's upset I've been given all the cred-it—er, accusation," he corrected himself hurriedly, clearing his throat.

Artemis frowned at her father, and Tommy was still extending the folded piece of paper. She recognized the peel-off, wax-paper-like segment of chess annotation. The yellowed portion adhered to the back of the official notes.

Artemis had already seen this note. Had seen the annotation. Had attempted to remember the game they'd played.

In her mind, she'd played the moves out, over and over and over again.

But the hidden message hadn't made sense.

Now, though, Tommy was jutting the thing toward her, insistently. She looked down, and Tommy muttered, "I was thinking at first Helen had given a clue for you. . ." He shook his head. "But she found me. She handed it to *me.*"

Artemis stared at her brother.

Tommy said, "So I thought of how *I* would interpret this." Suddenly, he pulled a lighter from his pocket, holding it up. And through the paper, through the ink and annotation, darker etchings were visible, illuminated by the sparks from the lighter.

CHAPTER 5

As Artemis leaned in, staring at the flickering light, Tommy muttered, "Helen was always giving me things like this when we were kids. Puzzles, games . . . and this time . . . she gave the letter to *me*. Not to you, Art. She gave it to me."

Tommy's voice carried a quavering quality as he spoke now, and he wasn't quite meeting Artemis' gaze. He let out a long breath, but then said, "And that's why I had to see you first . . . before you nixed him." He jammed a thumb toward Otto.

Artemis was no longer looking at her family members, though. Instead, she was staring at the dark lettering now appearing on the paper itself. She frowned, shaking her head and saying, "Is that. . ."

Letters, she realized.

There, hidden in the annotation, emphasized only by the secret ink which the fire was causing, she read a simple phrase.

And as she read it, chills went down her spine.

Investigating the Ghost-killer. . .

It isn't dad.

She blinked, staring, then shaking her head side to side. Tommy watched her. Otto, always a master of reading human body language, said, "What is it? What did you find?"

But everyone had questions now. Everyone was confused.

Artemis reread the line.

Investigating the Ghost-killer. . .

It isn't dad.

She hesitated briefly, shaking her head side to side. "No. . ." she murmured. "No, that can't be right."

She looked up, but Tommy was staring straight at her. "See why I had to chat before you traded him?" Tommy shrugged. "Helen gave me this, Art."

"No," Artemis said firmly. "No, she couldn't have." Artemis' head shifted violently side to side.

But Tommy waved the paper toward her, the lighter still lifted in his other hand. He extended it at her once more, as if in some sort of invitation.

She didn't want to look. Couldn't bring herself to.

43

Tommy was scowling. *Investigating the Ghost-killer...*

Helen was looking for him? But... but how did...

Artemis stared at her father, trying to make sense of it all. Trying to piece it together. Information spun through her mind. Mr. Kramer had visited her father in prison, hadn't he?

She remembered what he'd said, could still recall the night she'd confronted him, the chill of the mountain air...

And Kramer's words...

"I visited your father in prison, you know," Kramer had said softly, his voice hoarse. *"He didn't have... No—no I hadn't seen it. Not at first. I spoke to the Ghost-killer. And that..."* he coughed, his knife shaking. *"That was where I found the path. Don't you see? The Ghost-killer helped me plan. Helped me execute. I couldn't have done this without the sheer genius—"*

It was subtle, but now she thought about it...

I visited your father in prison, you know...

He didn't have...

What?

What Kramer had wanted?

And then... I spoke to the Ghost-killer.

Not the same claim. *Your father.* The Ghost-killer.

44

As if they'd been two separate people. Kramer hadn't thought much of Artemis' father. All along, she'd assumed it had been rivalry, or jealousy. One killer matching against another.

But what if. . .

What if it had been disappointment?

What if Kramer *had visited* her father, and her father had said what he'd been saying for years now?

I'm innocent.

Kramer would've left, then. Would've looked elsewhere . . . and by the sound of things . . . he'd eventually found the Ghost-killer himself.

She was shaking her head side to side, though, still staring at the piece of paper gripped in Tommy's hand. Her father was a manipulator, a liar. He'd threatened his own daughter. . .

But when she thought back to those visits in prison—how many times had his threats and manipulation come *after* she'd refused to believe his innocence. He'd always claimed it. She'd always ignored him. And then he got irate.

As she considered this, though, more thoughts arose to the surface of her mind. She knew her father had also used drugs laced into postcards to manipulate guards . . . to manipulate prisoners. . .

"You have to be," she said suddenly, rounding on her father. "What about Joseph Baker?"

"What about him?" her father shot back.

"You were using him as a courier, a go-between—he was sending you postcards laced in hallucinogens!"

Her father winced, scratching at the side of his face. He still looked haunted and kept glancing at the phone in her hand. But after a moment, as if sensing the shifting winds, he refocused on his daughter, and his eyes narrowed. He watched her quietly and then began to speak. "I don't think you understand, Artemis. . ."

He spoke slowly, a cold edge to his words. He frowned at her and took a step toward her. No one intervened this time, so he dusted himself off and faced her fully now. He said, "I had to survive in there, didn't I? No one believed me. I was framed for murder. You thought I did it. So did Tomboy, over here."

Tommy just watched from behind those sunglasses, clutching his fluttering parchment like a flag. Artemis kept glancing toward the paper, trying to clear her head.

Was Tommy lying about seeing Helen?

No . . . no, what would he lie for?

He'd told her weeks ago. Had told her about Helen at the waterfall. Years ago, but *after* she'd supposedly disappeared. About three years *after* Helen had vanished, she'd given him a note.

He'd sworn it was her.

And the chess annotation, the hidden writing. . . Who else would it have been?

Investigating. . .

Helen had been looking into the Ghost-killer. And if Otto really *was* innocent, did that mean the real Ghost-killer had hurt Helen?

What if she'd found him?

Helen Blythe was the smartest person Artemis had ever known. Helen had been Artemis' tutor, her instructor.

So what if Helen had used those smarts and found the Ghost-killer? Found the man targeting young women like herself?

And what if. . .

It had all ended poorly?

What if Helen had disappeared *because* she'd wanted to avoid the Ghost-killer? What if she'd known someone had been obsessed with her. Someone had been hunting girls like her. What if. . .

But there were so many what-ifs. . .

Fake-Helen was involved now too. But if Otto hadn't hired her . . . then what game was *she* playing at?

And none of this helped Jamie or Sophie.

So Artemis just watched her father, leveling her gaze on him, listening intently as he spoke in rapid pace.

The man she'd always believed was the Ghost-killer was saying, "Almost two decades of my life were taken from me . . . so yes . . . yes perhaps I did *play* the game inside. I made some friends. I had leverage." He shrugged. "It gained me information, allies. Someone like me, in a place like that? I needed allies." He spoke quickly, almost defiantly.

"You threatened me," Artemis murmured. "You threatened to send some of your friends to hurt me."

"Did I?" He paused, then shook his head, releasing a sigh. "I . . . I may have gone too far. But you didn't believe me!" he retorted, scowling. "I tried kind. I tried begging. I tried pleading. But you never believed me. My own *daughter*!"

She stared at him, frozen in place, her blood bruiting through her veins, her heart pounding. She wasn't sure what she was supposed to say. What she was supposed to *do*. Her father had spoken like this before. On multiple occasions.

But now . . . she scowled at him, closing her eyes and massaging the bridge of her nose. Now . . . she was listening for the first time.

"They framed Art for murder, too," Tommy said, waving a hand at her.

Her father beamed now. "Did *they*?"

"They?" Artemis snorted. "For all I know, it was you. Is that it? Making me suffer like you did?"

Otto took a step forward, his hand extended as if to touch hers. Two paces away, he didn't approach fully, though. He must've seen the warning look in her eyes. She had no desire to be touched by this man. No desire for. . .

But . . . what if he wasn't?

What if he truly *wasn't* the Ghost-killer?

He was a manipulator . . . a liar. . . Others had all suspected Otto of being the Ghost-killer. Everyone knew it. The evidence. . .

She waved her hand, shaking her head. "No, no, no. We *saw* you. One of your victims in bed. Tommy—you saw that footage, you *did*!"

Otto yelled suddenly. "No!" he exclaimed, as if he could sense his influence suddenly slipping. He skipped forward, standing between his two children, arms spread as if attempting to intercept something. "No!" he repeated, louder, his voice retorting like a gunshot. "It was a plant. I was drugged. They *refused* to check my blood! I told them I'd been drugged. But Dawkins . . . the bastard," Otto scowled, hand bunching, "He didn't want to hear it. Still grieving the loss of his sweet, sweet wife. Such a pretty, kind woman. . ." Otto trailed off for a moment, frowning. But he looked up again, realizing the attention of his children, swallowing and continuing, "I . . . er . . . what was I saying? Oh—yes . . . yes, that's right. They didn't check it. But I was drugged. The corpse—that poor lady was put in the bed while I was sleeping!" He shivered, shaking his head and wringing his hands.

"I still sometimes have nightmares," he murmured in a trembling voice.

Now Artemis was shaking her own head, still staring at her father, but feeling a rising sense of horror within. "I . . . it's not real. It can't be," she muttered. "There's no way. . . There was a body in your bed!"

"Said he was drugged," Tommy shot back.

She rounded on him, "Since when did you believe *him*!"

Tommy waved the parchment with the secret message.

Helen.

It all came down to Helen.

She'd been investigating the Ghost-killer. She'd disappeared afterward. And she . . . if Tommy was to be believed . . . had claimed her father was innocent.

"The handwriting," Artemis said suddenly. "Let me see it!" She reached out, clicking her fingers. Tommy wrinkled his nose at her, but she snapped her fingers more insistently, and he hesitantly handed the parchment over to her as if it were more precious than diamonds.

"Don't tear it," Tommy warned.

She delicately took the annotation note and stared at the message. Her brow furrowed, and she reached back in her own memory, sifting through the photographic images that she stored in her mind. Some called it a photographic memory, to Artemis it was rapid recollection.

She could remember the time she'd gone camping with Helen. . . The kidnapper, this psychotic woman, had brought up the color of the damn tent. . . Artemis could picture it too. She could also picture notes that the two girls would occasionally pass each other while fishing in the small family canoe with Tommy.

Sometimes, their brother had lost his temper to the point that the only way to chat without irritating him was to hand notes.

Helen had been considerate like that. Always looking out for her younger siblings, even though she was the eldest.

Now, Artemis brought to mind one of those notes, passed from one hand to the other.

She frowned as she pictured it, bringing the letters to mind. Tommy had been given this note not long after Helen had disappeared.

The letter "g" had a strange swoop to it. The handwriting, unlike most things in Helen's life, was messy.

And it was also a perfect match.

Artemis kept the image surfaced in her mind while simultaneously staring at the note with the invisible ink.

A match.

An *exact* match.

It was Helen's handwriting. Not only that . . . but as Artemis' breath came in slow, shallow gasps, she recognized the annotation as well.

A game they'd once played on the river, in that same canoe, fishing. Playing chess in the back of the boat while Tommy cast his line.

A game that Artemis had won—in fact, one of the only games she'd *ever* won. Artemis frowned, wondering why the chess annotation was of *that* particular game.

Artemis' mind extended, moving back. . .

And then she paused, staring at the ground, exhaling faintly.

She remembered that day. Years ago. . . Remembered Tommy's foul mood. Remembered notes handed back and forth. Remembered her first victory over her sister.

And could remember their conversation.

The two of them sitting, their legs folded primly in the boat, Artemis only nine, Helen five years older at fourteen. Artemis had won. Helen toppled her queen in resignation following a revealed attack on the queen. . .

And Artemis had said, "You look distracted, Helen."

Her sister's bronze curls had framed her features perfectly, and Helen had glanced over at Artemis, a far-off look in her eyes.

She had just shaken her head and said, "I . . . I found something yesterday. At the house. . ."

"What did you find?"

But Helen hadn't answered and instead had smiled, reaching out and patting her younger sister on the arm. "Nice opening, by the way!" Helen had said, cheerful all of a sudden. "You killed me!"

Now, standing in the junkyard, Artemis remembered the exchange. Even the unfortunate use of the word *killed* to reference outplaying in a game of strategy.

But Helen had been distracted. . .

Was there something about that game Helen had wanted Artemis to remember?

Artemis shook her head, committing the annotation to memory, before glancing at Tommy and murmuring, "It's her handwriting. It's Helen's."

Tommy nodded. "I told you."

"But . . . he's not . . . that's not. . ." Artemis turned, scowling at her father now.

He watched his children, wearing a curious, inquisitive expression. But he still had that same wolfish quality to his features. He had always been a liar. He'd always been a manipulator. None of that changed. . .

But this was Helen's handwriting. This was Helen's note.

And now, Artemis realized something else. . .

The reason the annotation was important.

"Oh. . ." she muttered out loud, feeling silly all of a sudden.

CHAPTER 6

Helen had used the annotation to *prove* it was her. It was like a passcode. A password with fifty different numbers and letters. Each move in the match had been *only* something Helen and Artemis had known. Tommy hadn't been watching, his back to the game while he'd fished and scowled at the scenic vista.

Only Helen and Artemis had known the game's moves.

And now there it was, on the same parchment where Helen had claimed she'd been investigating the murders. . .

And so, Helen *had* to have sent this.

And Fake-Helen, the kidnapper, didn't know anything about it.

Artemis paused, leaning in now, speaking quiet, slow, so only Tommy could hear. Her heart was pounding, but she said, "I need to rescue Jamie."

"We can do that," Tommy replied. "The meeting is tomorrow, yeah?" he glanced at the dark clouds above, at the nighttime sky. He shrugged, looking back at her. "Nothing you can do until you rendezvous anyway."

Artemis nibbled on her lip. This was true. Until she met with the kidnapper, in order to make the trade, she would just be twiddling her thumbs.

And in the meantime. . .

She glanced toward her father.

Innocent?

He'd claimed it for years . . . forever. Despite the overwhelming evidence.

But now, Helen agreed.

Innocent.

Artemis glanced back at Tommy. "Can you . . . can you keep an eye on him?" she said, still murmuring.

"What was that?" Otto called out.

But Tommy replied, also quiet, "Sure. I'll tie him up if you'd like."

"Yeah. Do it. I don't want him sneaking off."

Tommy flashed a thumbs up. Frowned. "What are you going to do?"

Artemis only had hours. . . Eight hours until she was due to meet up with the kidnapper. Eight hours to figure out this mess, to untangle it all.

And so, she closed her eyes, considered her options, then took and folded the annotation neatly.

"Hey, that's mine," Tommy said.

Artemis nodded toward Otto. "And that's mine. Trade. I need this, if I'm going to solve it, I need it."

"Solve what?"

"The Ghost-killer's murders," Artemis said simply, looking her brother in the eye. She refused to glance in her father's direction. She said, "If he's innocent . . . then the killer is out there. The kidnapper said she worked for the Ghost-killer for a while. And Helen. . ." Artemis patted her pocket with the folded note. "Helen was investigating the killer . . . if she found him. . ."

"Then maybe he's the one who did something to her. Killed her? Maybe that's why she's in hiding!" Tommy said suddenly, eyes wide. "Maybe she's being hunted and doesn't want to put any of us in danger!"

Artemis stared at the excitement in her brother's expression. She felt a similar rising sense of hope at this suggestion. She didn't know if it was even possible. . . Certainly didn't know if it was true.

But instead of conjecture, Artemis wanted to deal in facts.

Cold, hard facts.

Helen was out there. Helen had sent the note.

Their father was possibly innocent. . .

Artemis glanced at him, frowning. He was smiling at her. She felt her skin crawl. . . But now, it was only partly due to his disingenuous expression.

And partly. . . The cold chill at realizing, if her father really was innocent, then he'd spent nearly two decades behind bars. *She* had hated the man for almost twenty years.

She stared at him, feeling her knees wobble now. A weakness suddenly swelling through her. She didn't want to consider it.

"Not until I prove it," she muttered to herself.

"What was that?"

"Nothing just . . . I . . . I'm not going to make any decisions until I prove it."

Tommy shrugged, adjusting his sunglasses. "But how?" he said simply. "You really think you'll be able to find the Ghost-killer?"

She sighed. "You really think he's innocent?" she murmured, keeping her voice low again.

"Yeah. Helen said so." He pointed at the note.

"It's as simple as that for you?"

"When was Helen ever wrong?"

"It's been a while, Tommy. . . We don't even know if she's still alive."

"Well. . . You better find out then."

Artemis nodded, wincing as she did. Her hand lifted, brushing at the back of her neck, feeling her skin strangely warm. She glanced along the junkyard, under the dark skies, standing in the night. And then she reached a decision.

"Only one place to start, isn't there?" she said.

"And what's that?"

"The evidence. The old case files."

"That'll be locked up tight," said Tommy, wrinkling a nose. "Need me to send someone with?"

"No. . . No, I'm not going to break in. I'm going to walk in."

"How?"

"I . . . I might have an insider willing to help," Artemis said. "At least . . . I hope so."

"Who?"

But Artemis was already turning, moving now. She pointed a finger at their father and quirked a brow at her brother, clearly signaling what she wanted.

"Yeah, yeah. He's not going anywhere," Tommy called after her.

Otto just frowned, opening his mouth to protest, but Artemis had turned fully and was stalking away now. One of the thugs moved to intervene, but Tommy clicked his tongue, and the large man backed away, like a hound called to heel.

And Artemis picked up her pace, still wearing almost-damp clothing, her hair a mess, her body exhausted, her eyes weary. . .

But her mind was alive, active, and spinning.

There was no rest for her mind.

And there wouldn't be any rest until Jamie and Sophie were safe and all of this was solved.

Was her father really innocent? Was Helen alive? Who was Fake-Helen, and who'd hired the kidnapper? Was Otto behind all of it, manipulating everyone?

She cursed as she picked up the pace, moving faster.

One step at a time.

Only one step.

First things first—she needed access to those old files. Files that would be stored in the small precinct of Pinelake.

In an evidence locker guarded by the police.

And by the Dawkins family, in particular. The Dawkins family had long hated Artemis' kin. The feud went back years... Ever since Abraham Dawkins, the sheriff, had lost his first wife to the Ghost-killer.

The Dawkinses blamed Otto, and blamed Artemis for not knowing what her father was.

It didn't matter to them that Artemis had only been ten years old at the time of the murders. It didn't matter to them at all.

But she needed to look at the evidence. She was tired of hearing talk. Of listening to *people*. Facts didn't lie. Evidence didn't lie.

But the only way to enter the precinct was if she got a little help.

And so, hastening down the junkyard road, she raised her phone to her cheek, uttered a small prayer, then made a call.

A lot was riding on this.

Artemis could only hope her contact was in a helpful mood.

CHAPTER 7

Artemis exhaled slowly in anticipation, her breath rising like steam. The taxi had dropped her off three blocks away, and she had walked from there.

Now, she peered toward the small police precinct in the center of an office complex. A couple of vehicles were parked in the cracked and fissured asphalt lot. It was well past midnight now, and the blue moon was peeking through the clouds, illuminating the lake with a vibrant sheen of lunar glow.

Artemis stood across the street, in the shadows of a tall tree.

The lake, only a stone's throw to her right, was surrounded by equally large trees, boasting long branches extending out to the sky.

She checked her phone.

1:32 A.M.

She remained motionless in the shadows of the tree, shivering faintly. She still wore the same sweater, the same dark sweatpants. The taxi driver had accommodated her request to turn the heat up, and now her outfit was dry.

She stared toward the light glowing through the glass doors of the precinct.

She did *not* have fond memories of the Pinelake police department.

Did not have fond memories of Sheriff Dawkins or his grandsons who worked as cops. Her stomach felt sour as she stared at the precinct, and she leaned against the tree, her shoulder brushing the bark.

"You can do this," she whispered to herself.

But even as she said it, she felt a jolt of fear.

She peered into the night, watching as a silhouette moved across the window, a dark outline illuminated against the glowing, orange backdrop of lighting through the window.

The office complex accommodated three other workspaces. One of them, to the left, was a boutique store. To the right, though. . .

She shivered.

The coroners.

Artemis picked up her pace, moving away from her shelter beneath the tree, fleeing the shadows, and hastening toward the coroner's office, moving rapidly as she did.

Her breath came rapidly as she took equally hasty steps over the asphalt, up the sidewalk, along the side of the two parked police vehicles, and toward the rear entrance leading into the coroner's office.

"Come on, come on," she murmured to herself as she walked forward.

She paused at the hood of one of the police vehicles, glancing over the car in the direction of the office, peering through the dark. Another figure had approached the first. It looked as if the two of them were engaged in conversation, both of them seemingly oblivious to Artemis' attention.

Was one of them a Dawkins brother?

She didn't want to find out.

But she had to get into the evidence locker, and so that meant she had to enter the precinct.

The coroner's office had an entrance that connected the two spaces. . . But it took a keycard and a passcode plus a fingerprint scan for entrance.

Artemis could only hope her accomplice would show up on time.

As she moved around the hood of the parked police cruiser, she heard a sudden *click*. Artemis' eyes bugged, and she whirled around, staring in horror toward the front of the parked car.

The door opened slowly, and a man pushed from the front seat, speaking into a phone. "No, no . . . all quiet on that front. We'll see. Just a five-minute stop. I'll be by."

The man had been sitting behind tinted windows. She'd watched his car for ten minutes before approaching, but by the look of things he'd been engrossed in his call.

She didn't recognize the cop, but she didn't wait to look long. Instead, she turned hastily, presenting her back to him and moving toward the coroner's office.

As she hastened away from the parked car, she kept checking her phone, attempting to watch the man in the reflection of the glass. She could feel her heart pounding, the fear rising in her body.

Could feel her stomach tightening as anxiety attempted to settle on her.

The cop shut the door to his car, still talking on the phone.

She kept walking.

He kept talking.

She kept w—

He went quiet.

She didn't stop. Didn't allow him any reason to think she'd been listening. He couldn't recognize her from *behind* surely. Her hair was uncombed, her outfit completely inconspicuous.

But the man cleared his throat, and then the cop behind her called out. "Hey, ma'am!"

She kept going.

"Excuse me, ma'am?"

She raised a hand as if in greeting, gave it a little flutter, but continued hastily on her path.

She couldn't look back, couldn't show her face. The cop would recognize it instantly. Her face was plastered on television now. The story of her murdering Azin had circled the news sites.

She was a wanted fugitive.

Agent Butcher, an FBI investigator, had been killed back at Jamie's farmhouse, and they suspected her of this murder as well.

"Ma'am!" The cop called, a bit louder now, his voice sharp.

She had reached the steps to the coroner's office, and paused, her hand lingering on the wooden rail. She didn't know what to do. By ignoring him, she was behaving suspiciously. She wished she hadn't waved at him, hadn't acknowledged him at all.

Now, all she could think to do was reach up and adjust at her ears, as if she were wearing headphones. She pretended to adjust one, then the other, flung her shoulders back as if preparing for something, then moved up the stairs.

To add to the farce, she even bobbed her head.

She wondered how her father might have sold the lie. A lie without a word. A lie through mimicry alone. Her father had always been a master interpreter of body language. And now, as she moved up the stairs, slowly, reaching the dark door of the coroner's office, she rocked her head back and forth while pressing at an ear, hoping the cop would buy the ruse.

She stared at her reflection in the dark glass.

And spotted the tall cop by the parked sedan staring straight at her. He was frowning and also peering at the reflection.

She ducked her head quickly. At the distance he stood at, though, she doubted he'd be able to recognize her based purely on a reflection.

Still, there was no point taking any chances.

"Hey. . . Do I know you?" the voice called out now, even more suspicious. He didn't even raise his voice, clearly not buying the fake-earphones trick. She supposed cops likely encountered similar deceptions as a regular occurrence.

She couldn't turn. She just stared at her reflection, resisting the urge to check her phone.

Come on. . . Come on. . .

And then, her heart jumped.

The cop was approaching her.

Slowly, now, but his thumb was hooked in his belt, his fingers tapping against the holster of his weapon. He took long strides, approaching her cautiously. His reflection in the glass drew closer, and he was staring straight at her.

She watched as he lowered his phone, and his other hand lingered on his walkie-talkie as if preparing to call in for backup.

She was frozen in place, using a dim reflection in dingy glass, parked at the top of a staircase, facing a door sealed with keycard and fingerprint technology.

Shit. Shit. Shit.

The mantra echoed in her head, rhythmically. In the same timing with the fake music she'd been mimicking.

The cop was now on the curb. Now at the base of the stairs.

And she couldn't do anything.

If she turned, he'd recognize her. If she tried to run, they were outside a police precinct. They'd hunt her down instantly. She didn't even have a car to retreat to—she'd taken a taxi.

She could feel herself hyperventilating.

Her hands tensed at her sides. . . His gun was still holstered.

She desperately poked at an ear again, still playing pretend.

"Ma'am!" snapped the cop.

She watched as he took a step up, reaching out a hand now, his fingers touching her shoulder. She wanted to scream, to turn.

She was frozen in place. Normally, Forester came with her on such excursions. She could always trust the FBI agent to have her back in a physical altercation.

But now?

Now she was isolated. Alone.

The cop's grip tightened, beginning to turn her.

CHAPTER 8

Suddenly, the dark, reflective door to the coroner's office flung open.

"Oh, Lord, *there* you are!" exclaimed an energetic voice which accompanied an equally brisk figure in the form of a well-proportioned woman with bright pink hair braided into intricate patterns. The woman was carrying a clipboard, wearing gloves and a white lab coat. She had something jutting out of one pocket, which looked suspiciously like a human arm bone.

But now, Dr. Miracle Bryant stepped forward, leaned in, wrapping Artemis in an embrace before pulling her, more like *dragging* her, through the open door.

"Dr. Bryant!" the cop called behind her.

But Miracle didn't respond at first. Instead, she pushed Artemis into the dark corridor of the coroner's office, away from the entrance to the door.

Artemis stood in the shadow of the walkway, trembling, arms wrapped around her form.

"Officer Peterson!" Bryant said. "How in the world are you doing, sweetie? You look downright exhausted—has it been a long day?" A snap of fingers, a lilt of the voice. "Oh, no, let me guess. Donna, again? I'm sorry, child—but I'll remember her in my prayers twice as much. If there's anything I can do—"

"Er, yeah, thanks, Dr. Bryant. Who was that woman in there with you?"

"Her? Oh—she's my deaf understudy."

"Deaf?"

"Mhmm," said Bryant.

And Artemis remained out of sight of the open door, in the shadow created by a concrete support beam, leaning against the cold wall and still trembling. She felt a flash of gratitude for Dr. Bryant's quick lie.

Deaf . . . perhaps that would convince the officer as to the reason for her ignoring his calls.

Then again. . .

Artemis winced, feeling her stomach twist.

"I . . . I'd like to speak with her," said the officer.

"Oh? Why's that?"

A pause. "She was standing near my car, and I'm concerned she was listening in."

"To your conversation? No, no dear. Donna, again?"

"No," said the officer a bit too quickly. He sounded sheepish. "Just . . . you're sure she's your assistant?"

"What are you afraid of, honey? A private investigator? Your wife wouldn't do that."

"Ex-wife!" he shot back.

"Right, right. Of course. Well, I can promise you, my assistant is too tired to talk right now. What about tomorrow morning?"

"What was her name again?"

A pause. A bit too long. Then Dr. Bryant cleared her throat and said, "Er. . . Art. . . Em . . . erson. . ."

"Art Emerson?"

Artemis winced.

"Yes!" Dr. Bryant said, still maintaining her veneer of ceaseless cheer. Meanwhile, behind her back, she kept waving a hand as if trying to direct Artemis further down the hall.

Artemis hesitated, frowned, and then began to slip along the wall, her shoulders scraping the smooth surface. Her head bumped a poster over one shoulder. She glanced back and spotted a cat dangling from a branch—the cat was wearing a sparkling party hat. And the poster read, *Hang in there!*

A few other motivational posters could be glimpsed lining the coroner's office on the opposite wall.

Artemis didn't slow to examine any of these. Her heart hammered as she listened to the voices still coming from the open doorway.

The hall turned off to the right. And sticking to the shadows, Artemis slipped along the wall, entering the right side and avoiding a doorknob jutting out against her back.

Dr. Bryant operated in more than one office, but Artemis had visited her in the Pinelake one before. Dr. Bryant had also been the only other person besides Forester to hear the voice of Fake-Helen over the phone. At the time, Miracle had been pointing a gun at Artemis and Cameron.

Now, she was—albeit tentatively—on the side of the fugitive.

Everyone else in the police department suspected Artemis of murder.

For now, Miracle was the only friend Artemis really had.

And the ultimate goal was still clear. Artemis needed entrance into the evidence room in the sheriff's department. There were police patrolling the offices—hopefully none of the Dawkins family. But regardless, if she wanted to find out who the *real* Ghost-killer was, to find out if her father was truly innocent of the crimes he'd committed.

. .

Then she had to solve the case herself.

She'd already solved a decades old murder involving a man who they'd called the Aristocrat.

Would this be any different?

Another shiver along her back as she avoided a second door opening which yawned into the room beyond. If she found the Ghost-killer. . . Would she find Helen?

Would she find out, even worse, that Helen was already dead?

If her sister had also been investigating this serial killer . . . what if the Ghost-killer had found out? What if he'd killed her sister? The other victims in the town had all been smart young women. Just like Helen.

What if Helen had fled because she'd *known* the killer might target her next?

"Too many what-ifs. . ." she murmured to herself, trying to center her thoughts.

And then, she heard Dr. Bryant bid farewell. A buzzing sound of a door locking and then the hurried sound of rapidly approaching footsteps.

There was a spry energy to the footsteps, though Dr. Bryant was a middle-aged woman with an ample frame. She had the feet of a dancer, evident in the rhythmic tapping as they now approached.

Dr. Bryant turned the dark corner, the sound of beads rattling from the shawl she wore over her lab coat. Two earrings swished from her ears, one the shape of a crucifix, the other evidently made of a macaroni spiral.

Dr. Bryant's eyeshadow was an impressive hue of green. And now the coroner had paused, clipboard in hand, still wearing her gloves as she studied Artemis in the dark.

The woman's usually cheerful personality had faded somewhat. Though she was still in possession of nervous energy which came out in the way her foot kept tapping against the floor.

"So..." Dr. Bryant said quietly, "What's this about? On the phone you said it was life or death."

Artemis nodded but glanced past the woman. "Is he gone?"

"Oh, umm, yes. He was just worried his wife had hired you to spy on him. It's nothing."

Artemis blinked, opened her mouth to ask further questions, closed it again, then released a sigh. She said, "Alright then..." She glanced down the hall, bit her lip, then murmured, "I need access to the evidence locker."

Dr. Bryant stiffened.

Artemis grimaced but pressed on. "I didn't tell you over the phone because I knew you'd think it was a bad idea, but hear me out."

Dr. Bryant watched Artemis, quiet and contemplative. Worry lines etched across her pleasant features, her dark complexion was cast in even deeper shadow by the dim lights of the hall, and the green eye-shadow stood out like neon.

Artemis couldn't quite meet the coroner's gaze. On her way over, she'd considered the best approach to broach the subject with Dr. Bryant. Now, standing there, brow furrowed, Artemis began, speaking quickly. "I know you're already out on a limb for me, but I have to go over old evidence on the Ghost-killer's case."

Dr. Bryant still said nothing.

Artemis soldiered on. "I know how it sounds," she said quickly. "Trust me, I know. But I *have* to. If I don't. . ." She winced, shaking her head and rubbing her hands together now. She then tried, "You heard the kidnapper's voice. Back in the apartment of your old friend. You *heard* the voice."

Dr. Bryant nodded once.

She'd been there when Fake-Helen had spoken. She'd been there to hear the threats, the maniacal tone. She'd ended up choosing to trust Artemis and Forester.

Now, though, Artemis could see the doubt in Dr. Bryant's eyes.

But she also *knew* this woman. Not well . . . but enough.

Dr. Bryant was loyal to her friends. Once she chose to trust someone, she went all in. It was what Artemis had seen back at the nursing home.

An older woman, an old friend of twenty years of Dr. Bryant. The woman, a Mrs. Solenger, had been trapped in that nursing home for more than a decade, but Miracle visited her twice a week. Reading to the woman sometimes, or playing games, or just spending time in each other's company.

Dr. Bryant lived on behalf of those she chose to take under her wing.

The woman had a positive attitude, loved slogans, wore macaroni earrings paired with religious emblems. She was an odd duck.

But also the only person in the entire town who Artemis trusted in that moment.

Artemis said, "My father might be innocent. . . I know that's a lot to hear. But Jamie is still in the clutches of the kidnapper. Sophie is still with him. I have only. . ." she glanced at her phone screen— "seven hours left before I'm supposed to meet them and make a trade." She winced, still rubbing at the hems of her sleeves, breathing hastily as she did. "Please," she murmured. "I need to find out what happened. I need to find the Ghost-killer."

"We found him," Dr. Bryant said carefully. "He's in prison."

Artemis didn't reply. It was still late. So far, no one had found out that Otto Blythe had escaped. The warden who'd delivered her father had likely hidden this fact from the guards and the others he worked with.

The warden was also a piece of work.

But Artemis couldn't solve the world's problems. She was just one woman. All she could do was her best.

And now, she was staring directly at Dr. Bryant, her gaze pleading. She didn't mention that her father was out of jail. She didn't think it would help her cause.

So instead, she said, "I need to find out who the Ghost-killer really is." She hastily added, "If it's Otto, then fine! That's fine. . . We'll prove what everyone already knew."

"And if not?" Dr. Bryant said cautiously. "Where is this information coming from anyway? Why suspect he isn't?"

Artemis shrugged once. "My sister. Helen. She contacted my brother. . . Told him some things. Just . . . I trust her." Artemis gave a little shrug. "I know . . . I know that it's been years, but I *know* Helen. I've always known her. She was my best friend growing up. I loved her more than anyone. And I trust her. I'd trust her tonight with my life if I had to."

Dr. Bryant merely watched Artemis, but at this part, she let out a faint sigh, massaging the bridge of her nose. She glanced over her shoulder, down the hall.

"I really shouldn't. . ." Dr. Bryant said quietly.

"I won't take anything else!" Artemis said quickly.

Most people would've been suspicious. Artemis was wanted for murder, after all. She was well outside the law, hiding from cops, and now asking for a coroner to help her break into the adjoining police precinct.

Dr. Bryant was well within her rights to shout for the police and let them handle Artemis.

But now. . .

Dr. Bryant was also an accomplice. She'd been *seen* with Artemis.

None of this seemed to register, though. Miracle wasn't narrowing her eyes in suspicion. Nor did she look worried, as if fearful she might be roped into all of this. The woman didn't seem like the frightened type.

Instead, she had crossed her arms over her ample chest, her clipboard extended off to the side, her tongue tucked inside a cheek. She frowned briefly, let out a long breath, and said, "Where I grew up. . ." She paused, frowning. "No one thought I would ever make anything of myself. College . . . graduate degrees. I was told I'd end up on a street corner somewhere." Dr. Bryant flashed a smile. "I believed them and acted like I believed them for years in my early teens."

Artemis stared at Bryant, eyes wide.

Miracle shrugged. "I've learned. . ." she said cautiously, "Over the years . . . that when *everyone* thinks something. . . It's worth a second look. That applies to you, and also the Ghost-killer." Dr. Bryant pursed her lips. "Tell me one thing, though."

"Anything?"

"Did you intentionally wait until you were seen with me to ask? In order to put me in trouble? If I turn you in now, I'll be arrested too. Did you know that?"

Artemis paused, staring. The woman didn't look away, but watched Artemis, her expression unreadable.

Artemis didn't know what else to do but tell the truth. So she said, "I knew it, yes. But that wasn't *why*."

Bryant studied Artemis a moment longer, then sighed. "I'll be praying for you, dear. Now come, tie me up."

Artemis froze. "Excuse me?"

"It has to look real, doesn't it? Plausible deniability." She held up a firm finger. "It isn't deception if it's *implied*!"

Artemis wasn't sure what this comment meant. She also didn't think it was intended for her ears so much as Miracle's own conscience.

And so, Artemis just shrugged. "Show me where to go—how to access the precinct. And I'll take it from there."

"Alright, dearest. Come, this way. Hurry."

Artemis winced, falling into step with Miracle as the coroner spun on her heel and moved, with dancer's feet, down the hall, urgency in every step.

As they moved, Dr. Bryant shot Artemis a look. "I'm trusting you," she said simply.

It was a short sentence, and yet it meant so much.

Artemis nodded back. "I'm telling the truth."

"I believe you," Miracle said softly, and there wasn't any doubt in that voice. But she added, "I'm trusting you. I'm not saying it for my sake. But for yours. You're worthy of trust, Artemis Blythe. Now here—just through this door. Use this card. My office is that room. Make the ropes tight, then use the card on that door. Got it?"

Artemis' emotions were all tangled like wires, but she just nodded quickly and listened intently to the instructions, her eyes tracking Miracle's finger which indicated the doors down the hall.

The largest of which led, through a metal frame with an electronic keypad, into the adjoining police station.

And into further danger.

CHAPTER 9

Artemis rubbed her hand against her leg, wincing from where the bristles of the rope had gouged into her skin. The door shut slowly behind her, giving a final glimpse of where she'd secured Dr. Bryant to the desk chair.

The coroner had even insisted Artemis knock over some of her desk ornaments and topple books off a shelf, which had included tomes like *Chicken Soup for the Soul* and *Fifty Knitting Designs for You!*

Now, the office looked as if it had been ransacked, the coroner as if she'd been mistreated.

Artemis was already in over her head, and she wasn't sure if the ruse would matter. But ultimately, she was already on borrowed time.

Rubbing her hand against her leg, wincing from the use of the rope which Dr. Bryant had procured from a toolbox under a gurney,

Artemis approached the indicated door separating the coroner's office from the precinct.

In one hand, Artemis clutched the keycard she'd been given by Dr. Bryant.

Her breath came in puffs, and her heart skipped. She approached the door, reaching out with the card and flashing it over the keypad.

A faint flash of a green light. A quiet *click*.

She gripped the cold metal handle, opening the door slowly.

As she did, she realized just how thick the metal door was. At least half a foot of steel. The bulletproof glass reflected her nervous expression back until the door had opened completely.

A slow chill crept through the divider between the two halls.

The air-conditioning from the precinct was far colder than the coroner's office space.

Artemis shivered faintly, feeling goosebumps erupt across her skin where she stood in the door. She swallowed hesitantly, peering into the dark space beyond.

As she glanced ahead, it appeared as if she was in a lower section of the police station. The walls were bare, unpainted. In addition, she didn't spot movement or the illumination of bright lights she'd seen from the parking lot.

Artemis hesitated, standing in the doorway, one foot still in the hall behind her.

She thought of the police officer who'd spotted her outside. He hadn't seen her face, but what if he had recognized her after all? What if there were police, even now, being called as backup to come investigate?

She shook her head, refusing to let her mind go there. The fear was settling in her stomach. She wanted to turn back, but that wasn't an option.

She needed to look at the old evidence.

And so, she stepped hurriedly into the dark, unpainted, gray hall. The bulletproof dividing door between the two spaces closed behind her.

As it did, she felt as if she'd been sealed in a tomb. Behind her, she spotted posters on the wall and on the back of the door, informing her of various procedures for requesting information from the coroner's office.

One handwritten note, in looping cursive and colored, glitter-filled letters simply read: *Please do not store lunch in the same refrigerators as the bodies. Thank you!*

Artemis studied this note for a moment, then turned away.

She began to move slowly, her eyes on the only set of stairs at the end of the far, dark, bare hall.

Something about the gray walls, the unpainted room made her think of what she was leaving behind. She thought of Dr. Bryant's studio and felt a shiver. She licked her lips slowly, moving forward, both hands tensed.

She reached the base of the stairs, listening intently. The evidence room would be on a lower level, wouldn't it?

But she didn't see any other branching halls, or doorways. Just the corridor leading to the stairs. She glanced back, wishing she'd asked for more detailed directions from the coroner. As it was, Artemis could feel the anxiety returning.

She wasn't accustomed to facing such excursions alone.

No more Forester for backup.

No one except Artemis.

"Come on," she whispered. "One step at a time. Just one."

She took the stairs like this, having to pause every few moments to give herself a chance to recover. And she moved up the stairs, cautiously, breathing in shallows puffs.

And that's when she spotted the light, turning around the lacquered wooden banister, the cold steps rigid underfoot. She heard voices above her.

She glanced through the open door at the top of the stairs, leading up from the basement hall, and she heard someone saying, "What did she look like?"

"Didn't see her face," came a second, familiar voice which she recognized as the patrolman's from outside. "But she was acting strange."

"Dr. Bryant knew her?"

"Said it was an assistant."

Artemis froze at the top of the stairs, one hand gripping the rail, her gaze attentive, searching for any cameras she might have to avoid. Through the open doors, she spotted an office area. Desks, chairs, dividers, and a few glass booths against the far wall.

In the reflection of the glass, she spotted three figures standing near one of the desks. A tall man leaned forward, resting his hands on the wood. Another man at his side had his arms crossed. Both of them faced the patrolman who'd been in the car, frowning by the looks of their expressions in the glass.

Artemis exhaled faintly, leaning with her back against the wall, peering into the room beyond. Her nose protruded just past the edge of the door. The stairs behind her seemed a welcoming thing, open and inviting. She wanted to turn and flee more than anything.

But the only path left to her was onward.

She exhaled slowly, summoning her willpower, and then eased around the corner of the door, keeping low.

And that's when she recognized the voices.

Her heart leapt. She took two steps, still stooped, lunging behind a barrier around one of the empty cubicles.

She was breathing rapidly now. . .

Just to double check, she peered around the flimsy divider once more, her gaze landing on the figures by the desk. They were only a few paces away from her, standing under the bright lights of a fluorescent bulb. All of them were frowning.

The tall man had shaved his head, leaving only a thin prickle of hair. He had a face like a stone slab, with blunt features and a bulging nose. His narrowed eyes only further added to the pug-faced picture.

This man, Ross Dawkins, was the younger brother of Merl.

Merl stood off to the side of Ross. Where Ross was large and oversized, Merl was whisker thin and wore glasses. He stood straight-postured, like a librarian, and watched as his younger, but larger, brother slapped a hand against his palm.

"You know Dad's orders," Ross snapped, referring to his father, one of the sergeants at the precinct who also hated Artemis' family. "Gotta keep an extra eye out. Something happened at Doler's Max security."

"The prison in Rechester?"

"Nah, town over."

"Shit—what?"

"Dunno yet," Ross replied. Now he was peering out the large floor-to-ceiling windows behind the patrolman, his gaze focused on the entrance to the coroner's office across the street.

Artemis had frozen stiff.

Ross was near her age, while Merl was a couple of years older. She'd known them both in school—back then, Ross had been exactly the sort of person his physical makeup might have connotated.

Merl, on the other hand, had been shy and too embarrassed to speak to girls. Once upon a time, he'd even asked her out.

But now, both of the Dawkins brothers loathed her.

They believed her father had murdered their grandfather's first wife.

She remained stooped, one hand braced against the cold, tiled floor, her back to the divider separating her from the men by the desk. She could feel her own anxiety swirling, could feel a desperate desire to turn and run.

But she had to see this through.

The men were still talking, but she tried to ignore them. Listening was only making her more scared. So instead, she began to glance over her shoulder, off into the other sections of the precinct. She breathed hesitantly, keeping her head low.

She couldn't stand and look to get her bearings, but the stairwell was to her back, and the main entrance beyond a set of metal detectors, bulletproof glass, and sliding doors was off to her right, ten paces away.

This gave her at least some sort of reference point. She frowned, then, still hunched, hidden out of sight; she closed her eyes.

It had been many years since she'd been dragged into this particular police station to be interrogated. But she could still remember the experience. Only a child at the time, and yet they'd treated her with contempt.

The tongue-lashing, the thinly veiled threats. . . It had all come from blame. They'd *blamed* her for not discovering what her father truly was.

And now. . .

She intended to do just that.

It still hadn't sunk in fully what it would mean if her father was innocent of the crimes he'd been accused of. She wasn't sure how she would take it.

One step at a time. . . She thought to herself.

Her eyes were still closed, fingers still splayed on the cold ground. And in her mind. . .

She went *back.*

Her thoughts retreating to another time. Another place.

More than fifteen years ago. She pictured the memory she'd stored. A memory she didn't often visit, as it hadn't been a very pleasant one.

But with a mind like hers, a memory like hers that played things as videos across her subconscious, she could pluck an event from any point in history. And so, she did just that, playing out the experience of being escorted into the police station.

She fidgeted, remembering the hand on her shoulder. The threats of Sergeant Dawkins, who'd had a droopy, brown mustache at the time, shoving her forward. She could remember the sirens behind her. The cold air-conditioning, even then.

The interrogation room came later . . . but she wasn't interested in that part.

Instead, she played the reel from her recollection of *entering* the building. She pictured everything: the layout of the desks had been different. No metal detectors. But there had been three rooms. One leading off to the offices. One leading further back, away from the main entrance. And one leading to the stairwell.

And . . . *there.*

She spotted a sign in the memory. A directory she'd passed on the way in.

Evidence had been in the room at the back.

She opened her eyes, breathing slowly, exhaling as she did. The evidence lockup was off to her left, but it would bring her across an open space between the desks. If she moved . . . they might see her.

And if she was spotted, it would all be over. She crouched still, trying to summon courage as she silently rotated on the floor, doing so tenderly so her shoe wouldn't squeak against the ground. Her cheek pressed against the divider, her fingers against the floor.

She exhaled faintly, slipping along the left side of the divider.

Five steps between her and a concrete support post. Then . . . beyond that, the door leading up a second flight of stairs.

She stared at it and realized she was holding her breath.

"Yeah, shit—might as well check," one of the men was saying.

She was only half paying attention.

Now, she heard movement. The three cops were beginning to disperse. *Shit.* Panic flared through her. If she moved now, they'd see her. But if she stayed put, they might just as easily spot her.

She could feel herself panicking. Her teeth pressed tightly together. A shadow spilled past her, as a figure moved directly toward her, coming from the opposite side of the divider.

She did the only thing she could think of: she ducked past the divider and dipped under the desk.

She hid in the shadows now, frozen in place. If the figure had spotted her, heard her, or noticed her on his way out, then she had effectively trapped herself like a rat in a cage. She remained there, hidden in the dark, motionless. Her breath came slowly in quiet puffs.

She remained frozen in place, tucked under the desk, her hands wrapped around her knees. She leaned back, her shoulders grazing the wood. Her gaze fixated on the shadow of the tall figure. A man paused in the doorway leading to the main entrance.

A tall man with a stone-slab face.

Ross Dawkins peered off in the direction of the evidence room, hesitating briefly. He paused, patting his hands against his chest, then pockets. The tall man cursed, glancing around, then turning. His silhouette was outlined, his shadow stretching past the chair into the dark where Artemis hid.

As he snatched something off the desk, there was the sound of jangling.

For a moment, Artemis' eyes bugged as she realized Dawkins was standing only a foot away from her. His jeans shifted—the tall cop was currently in casual wear. The last time she'd seen him, she'd been breaking into his house.

Dawkins snatched something else off the desk, muttering. "Hang on, hang on, I'm coming," he snapped. "Go on—I unlocked it."

There was the sound of a sliding glass door, and a second figure disappeared behind Ross, through the front doors.

The man's knees pointed at her. If she'd wanted, Artemis could've reached out and untied his shoes. But she didn't want to do anything but stay motionless, frozen in place, breathing slowly.

She didn't blink, barely even dared to breathe.

CHAPTER 10

Ross turned again, moving on his heel and hastening away from her once more. He was shoving something into his pocket as he went.

It was a small-town sheriff's office. Not the sort like in one of the big cities.

And so, only the single officer remained behind now. She could hear him pacing on the other side of the desk, near the windows.

The sliding glass doors whooshed shut as Ross and his brother exited. Artemis waited a few seconds longer, counting slowly in her head.

The cop by the window would undoubtedly watch the Dawkins brothers enter their vehicle. It was human nature to study motion.

And so, she turned and began to move.

Artemis hastened away from the desk now, moving quietly, slowly. Five paces. Four. Three.

She shot a glance back. The patrolman by the window was beginning to turn. Headlights flashed through the glass, and she heard the muffled sound of an engine starting.

Two steps. One.

She darted behind the concrete column, breathing heavily. And there, she spotted a glass door. Beyond it, two neatly arranged signs on the wall. One read, *Sheriff's*. With an arrow pointing up. The other with an arrow pointing down. *Evidence.*

She stared at the two white arrows, each one beckoning her like an offer to heaven or hell.

She shot a look over her shoulder now, peering back in the direction of the main room. Then, when she decided the patrolman was still distracted by the Dawkins brothers in the parking lot, she turned and burst toward the stairs leading down.

It was like a release of pent-up emotion. Her feet kept rhythm with her pounding heart, taking the stairs two or three at a time, flying down them as if she had Forester's lanky stride.

Up above, she spotted a camera, over the evidence door.

But too late. They'd see her on video. She ducked her head anyway, just to buy time, and pulled the security badge Dr. Bryant had given her.

She flashed it over the electronic pad by the door and then watched the green light spark, heard the satisfying click.

She let out a little gasp of triumph and then leaned her shoulder against the metal frame, pushing it inward.

She was out of time. She'd already passed under a security camera, and now she was stepping into a room with only one exit.

She couldn't be found. Not now.

Too much was counting on this.

She needed to find the evidence from the Ghost-killer's case.

And she needed to hurry.

She shut the door quietly behind her, wincing as it made a rattling sound that she could've sworn was far too loud in the silent station.

She tensed, listening, but no response.

Then, she spun on her heel, turning to face the evidence room. The door was shut behind her once more—the solid metal surface shielding her from view. Standing there, inhaling slowly, she felt a slow sense of relief fall over her.

Artemis leaned back briefly, her back to the door, her heart pounding in her chest as she surveyed the room in front of her. The evidence room was located on the second floor of the police station, and it was undoubtedly strictly off limits to anyone who wasn't a member of law enforcement.

But Artemis' desperation filled her with the fuel she needed. The cold metal of the door against her neck sent chills down her spine. She pushed off the door, exhaling slowly, and glancing around the room.

The rows of shelves were lined with numbers and letters denotating case files. She frowned briefly, murmuring to herself. Then said, "Bigger number, older case. . ." She paused, then quickly shook her head. "No, no don't be stupid." The smaller numbers, if labeled sequentially, would be the older cases.

Artemis turned to the right, moving toward where arrows—like signs in a library—directed to the smaller digits. The shadowy corner of the large room had dusty, tall shelves, further suggesting the age of the contents.

Off to the side, a thin, barred window, the sort that might only be found in a small town's evidence room, surveyed the road beyond. The streets were deserted, and the only sounds were the occasional car passing by and the distant barking of a dog. Artemis took a deep breath, gathering her courage, and then moved with surefooted steps.

She reached the furthest row of shelves, glancing along. But most of these shelves were empty. And the items she *did* spot looked even older than she was. She moved past a couple more rows of lockers until she paused, peering down another aisle. More content on these shelves. . . Paraphernalia, firearms. Bagged and tagged sundry. She moved along this row now, searching desperately.

The case number was seared into her mind, of course.

She remembered it from her first trip into this station, all those years ago.

2102.

She scanned the contents. 2231. 2222.

"Come on. . ." she murmured to herself. "Come *on*!" she insisted.

She slipped along the wide corridor between the shelves, her footsteps echoing in the empty hallway. She crept forward, her heart racing as she searched the rows of dusty evidence. Small plastic containers, old weapons long abandoned. No . . . nothing here. Not that . . . nor *that*. She scowled, still moving.

2201. 2190.

She kept moving.

And then stopped, staring. She swallowed faintly, eyes fixated on the last slot of the furthest shelf in the darkest, dingiest corner of the metal compartments.

2102.

The number she remembered.

Her father's case.

The Ghost-killer's case.

She stared, frowning. The elation she'd felt at spotting the number was slowly replaced by a sinking sensation in her stomach.

She'd found it at the end of the corridor but now faced a large metal safe with a keypad lock. A thick, black, steel box rested on the shelf, the keypad facing her. Artemis cursed under her breath. She reached out, fingers touching the cold surface of the safe, then glanced back down the hall.

No sign of the police. No sound of their voices.

Not yet.

She huffed a second, then hastily rummaged through her pocket, pulling out the small keycard Dr. Bryant had provided. She pressed it against an old magnetic strip.

Nothing happened.

"Of course not," Artemis muttered. "Of *course* not."

She paused, still staring at the safe, then shrugged, reaching out to try and open it.

It remained locked.

She supposed that would've been too easy.

She stared for a moment longer, let out a slow, fading breath, and felt a sinking sensation. "Think. . ." she muttered to herself. "*Think*!" she said, more insistently.

She tried to shift the safe, but it was too heavy—nearly the size of a microwave and clearly bolted to the metal shelf.

She glanced at the case number on peeling sticky tape beneath the safe, but it hadn't changed. She'd found the correct shelf. . . But the files were hidden.

Why?

She wondered.

She frowned, glancing along the shelves, and realized that a few other cases *also* had additional layers of protection. She couldn't make rhyme or reason of it but decided that wasn't the point anyway.

Whatever the obstacle . . . she needed what was in this safe.

For one wild moment, she wondered if it would be possible to steal the entire thing, cart it off to Tommy, and let her brother's criminal persuasions aid in this endeavor.

But then she stopped, hesitating.

"Tommy. . ." she muttered to herself, fishing her phone out hastily. She placed the call, pressing the device against her cheek and tapping a foot on the floor.

Sweat beaded on her forehead as she waited, her mind racing as she tried to think through all the possibilities of opening the safe, while also keeping an ear out for any approaching cops.

Finally, after what felt like an eternity, she heard a cleared throat and her brother's voice. "You good, sis?" said the curt tone.

"Yeah, Tommy, listen I've got. . ." she paused, trailing off. Then, unable to help herself, she said, "Is Dad still there?"

"Yeah. He's on ice."

She hesitated, swallowed, but when her brother added nothing more, she said, "Not—not *literally*, or do you—"

"No, sis," he snorted. "We've got him. He's fine. Where are you?"

She paused, her lips itching from the buzz of her whisper. She glanced once more down the corridor and was struck again by how silent everything was. She swallowed faintly, then said, "I've got a safe."

"What type of safe?"

"Umm. . . Like an old one."

"And you're calling me?"

"Yeah."

Tommy snorted. "Evidence safe?"

"Umm, yeah . . . why?"

Her brother snickered.

"Tommy . . . *why*?"

He cleared his throat, and she was reminded once again of the smiling-eyed, mischievous younger brother she'd grown up with. Until life had kicked the shit out of him and turned mischief to bitterness. Now, her brother's humor tinged his voice as he said, "Mighta had a small cap on that place."

"A what? Speak non-mobster." She was lowering her head now, shoulder down, speaking quietly to further muffle her voice.

Tommy said, "Might have had someone slip in and tamper in there. The safes were Sheriff Abe's doing."

"Wait, so you mean my evidence is locked in a safe because you and your goons stole something from the cops?"

Tommy snicked. "Nah, from next door."

Artemis frowned, looked up, glancing at the safe, then down again. "The coroners? What did you steal from the coroner's?"

"Don't worry. The safes I heard about. For some of the more high-profile cases—Abe wanted to keep things in house."

"Don't need a history lesson, Tommy. I just need what's in here."

Her brother's tone sobered a bit, then he said, "Alright, listen here. Gonna need you to tell me, is it a ZX-T or is it a ZX-Y."

"What?"

"Read the number to me on the side."

"Oh, yeah, umm— *T*. It's the T."

"Good, easy enough."

"Tommy, I don't have any tools," she said hurriedly.

"No need, just use the factory reset."

"The what?"

"Shit safe, Artemis. Meant for home use, not for cops. Abe's cheap. Try 8-2-1-3," he rattled off.

She did. The safe blinked, and an orange light flashed above the numbers.

"It didn't work!" she said.

"Alright, calm down. Try . . . 9-1-3-2."

"What's that?"

"Second factory option."

She tried it, each button emitting a beep as she pressed. But again, the orange light flashed and the door stayed closed.

"Huh, not working?" he said.

"No," she whispered back.

And then she heard the sound of movement. Muffled still, on the other side of the evidence room's door, but approaching. The steady tap of footsteps. Her heart twisted in her chest, and she wanted to turn and hide.

"Tommy!" she whispered fiercely. "Anything else?"

"Nah," he replied. "The thing locks for an hour on three fails."

"It *what*?" she snapped.

But Tommy was muttering to himself. Then he said, "Alright, we might just have to go hardware. Any chance you brought an acetylene torch?"

"What? No, I don't have. . ." But Artemis trailed off, frowning, staring at the safe. Her phone still gripped in her hand but now hung limply to the side as she stared distractedly.

Her heart was pounding heavily, and she was listening for the sound of an opening door. But for the moment, she leaned in and murmured, "So Sheriff Abraham Dawkins put these in?"

"Yeah."

"And they're not factory numbers?"

"No, unless you entered the numbers wrong."

"I didn't," she said.

Tommy muttered.

But Artemis said to herself, "I wonder if. . ." She reached out, finger hovering. And then she entered four digits, moving rapidly.

"What's that sound? Shit—you trying again?" he demanded.

But Artemis clicked the final number, hit the pound button, and suddenly the green light flashed. The door clicked.

And swung open . . . slowly.

She stared and felt a tingle down her spine, waving a hand vaguely to clear dust particles swirling in the air.

"What happened?" he was saying. "Artemis? Did it work? What was it?"

She murmured, "The anniversary date with his first wife."

"Oh. . ." Tommy trailed off.

They were both thinking the same thing, no doubt. The sheriff's first wife, the victim of the Ghost-killer, was still the love of his life. Everyone in town had known it. And now, using the date of his marriage with her as the code for the safe. . .

The same safe where the evidence for the Ghost-killer was kept. . .

Artemis wasn't sure what it hearkened, but she doubted it was anything good.

Still . . . she had to hurry. She reached in, snatching two folders and a small black zip-up bag shaped like a dopp kit.

Her hands were trembling. She issued a quick, "Thanks, but I gotta go," over the phone before hanging up and pocketing the device.

And then she turned, holding the two folders and the dopp kit close.

CHAPTER 11

Her fingers shook, and she peered ahead, down the hall.

The room was filled with shelves upon shelves of evidence, ranging from drug paraphernalia to weapons to stolen goods, and yet there weren't many places one might hide.

She clutched the dopp kit, her hands shaking as she opened it and rummaged through the contents. She felt something cold against her fingers. But before she could examine it, there was a sudden buzz then a *click*.

She froze, staring. A figure was moving on the other side of the evidence room door, judging by the long stretch of glowing orange light now introduced into the dark, dingy space of the room she found herself in.

She had to act fast. She couldn't risk being caught in the evidence room, and she knew that she would have to find a way to get the evidence out of the police station without being detected.

She slipped the bag into her waistband, gripping the folders.

The door had now swung open completely. She stared, her heart hammering.

The long shadow of a familiar figure now stretched into the room. Her eyes darted desperately toward the window with the bars over it. But there was no way through it. The bars were as thick as her fingers but spaced as wide as her hands.

She was a slim woman but not *that* thin.

Now, she leaned back, breathing heavily, head resting against the wooden shelf.

Footsteps approached. A low voice, soft and quiet... A familiar voice.

The voice of Ross Dawkins—he'd come back from the parking lot. He was alone by the look of things, his shadow moving into the evidence room ahead of him.

And now, quietly, the man with the crude-featured face began to speak, saying, "The funniest thing..." His voice shook faintly, carrying a sort of hidden emotion. Another footstep as he moved deeper into the evidence room.

There was a pause and a slow swallow.

For a moment, Artemis just stood frozen, back against the tall shelf. At her side, she spotted an old, rusted knife which had been left inside a bag. After a few seconds, much to her horror, she realized the knife wasn't *rusted* but rather rust-hued due to the old, dried blood left on the blade.

She shifted slowly, moving her arm away from the bag, her elbow away from the shelf.

The silence was almost worse than the original sounds, now that she knew someone was with her. But as she remained quiet, listening and scarcely breathing, she heard the sound of heavy breaths.

The labored breathing came from the other side of the shelf and caused more shivers to tremor up her spine.

"I saw you on camera," came the voice suddenly, and it had that same tremor of emotion.

The words took a second to register, but once they did, her heart nearly collapsed like an imploding star into a black hole.

"Where are you, Artemis Blythe?" said Ross Dawkins in that nasty, sneering voice of his.

She couldn't help herself now as hyperventilating breaths came rapidly. She peered through the gap in the metal shelves, over another, smaller locker at waist height. Through the items, and through gaps in the back of the metal shelving, where screws might have gone if the shelf had been secured to a wall, she spotted a shadow moving slowly.

Ross Dawkins knew she was in here.

She was alone, locked in an evidence room with *Ross Dawkins*. He'd shut the door behind him on purpose, it seemed, if only to trap her with him.

And now, as she considered her potential fate, shivers tremored along her arms, and her fingers felt cold where she pressed them into a fist against her own palm.

He'd come here alone. . .

He'd seen her on the cameras but hadn't called *anyone*.

And that was when she spotted the gun in his hand—visible through an anchoring opening in the back of the shelf. The tall, mean-mugged cop had his weapon drawn, his finger on the trigger. In a brief glimpse, having leaned forward, her breath still coming in quick puffs, she spotted sweat prickled across Ross Dawkins' doughy forehead.

He gripped his gun tightly, and there was something in his eyes she just vaguely glimpsed that unsettled her.

Ross hadn't asked for backup because he wasn't here to arrest her.

The Dawkins family had always hated her.

And now, following an evening only a few days ago when she'd broken into Ross' house in search of evidence of a different kind, she was trapped in this room with him.

He continued to breath heavily, murmuring, "Ms. Blythe. . ." He spoke in a sing-song voice. "I know you're in here. . ."

Chills continued to tremble down her spine.

She knew she couldn't possibly fight her way past the officer, but she also knew that she couldn't just give up.

She waited, and he peered along another rack—empty. But now he was moving toward her.

"Of course. . ." he muttered suddenly, his eyes darting up. "Here to destroy evidence, hmm?" he called out. "Is that it?"

She winced, waiting in place.

He took another step forward, his shadow stretching toward her.

Artemis had two options: to shrink back, hide in the shadows, and hope he passed. . .

But this wasn't an option at all. He was here for *her* after all—here to cause her harm. And so, she made the only choice she could; she made a split-second decision. Instead of shrinking back, she met him head on.

Fear pumping through her, horror in her heart, she held back a scream and moved *fast*.

She didn't retreat but rather waited until he rounded, until he was too close to aim. . .

And then she lunged past him, her shoulder colliding with Ross, sending him tumbling.

He yelled as he tried to snatch at her. His voice echoed like a gunshot behind her. His weapon, on the other hand, she'd been aiming for with her shoulder. As she collided with it, he yelled, but his hand hit the shelf, the bone catching metal.

A sound of a skittering weapon hitting the floor.

And then Artemis was moving too fast for him. She'd caught him by surprise, and there were no *actual* gunshots that followed. She could hear him shouting behind her, but she didn't stop. She flung open the evidence room door, using Bryant's keycard. She heard Ross cursing and briefly glimpsed him scrambling on the ground, trying to grab his gun where it had fallen.

But then, when he spotted her getting away, he abandoned the weapon—which had lodged under a shelf—and with a howl, came running after her.

She didn't wait to chat. Artemis sprinted down the hallway, her feet pounding against the floor as she raced toward the exit.

But then she spotted the patrolman from earlier standing near the sliding doors. He was blinking dumbly, staring in her direction.

She cursed, swerving toward the stairs, still gripping the folders, and sprinting *back* into the basement.

As soon as she stepped foot into the dimly lit basement, she knew she was in trouble. Her heart pounded in her chest as she tried to stay one step ahead. But now, she was trapped.

She could hear the heavy footsteps of Ross coming closer and closer, and she knew she had to act fast. She scanned the room, looking for anything she could use as a weapon. Her eyes fell upon a metal pipe lying in the corner, and she lunged for it.

As the cop rounded the corner, down the stairs, cursing her name, Artemis felt the rusty grit of the pipe in her hand. This time she waited, tense, and as he rounded the bottom step, she swung the pipe with all her might. It connected with a satisfying *thud*, and the cop went down with a groan. But she knew he wouldn't stay down for long.

Ross gripped at his head, stumbling, but he was twice her size and ten times as furious.

She ran to the other end of the basement, her feet pounding against the concrete floor. She could hear the cop struggling to his feet behind her, and she knew she had to keep moving. She spotted a door on the far wall and made a beeline for it.

She grabbed the handle and pulled, but it was locked. Panic began to set in as she heard the cop's footsteps getting closer and closer. She looked around frantically, trying to find another way out.

That's when she saw it—a small window high up on the wall. It was her only chance. She grabbed a nearby bench and stood on it, trying to reach the window. It was just within her grasp, and she managed to push it open.

She hoisted herself up and through the window, her legs kicking wildly as she tried to get through the small opening. She could feel Ross' hand on her ankle, trying to pull her back, but she was determined.

With a final burst of strength, she wriggled loose, terror flooding through her, but she tumbled out onto the grass outside. She was free.

Gasping desperately, she struggled to her feet and took off running, not looking back until she was several blocks away.

Now, sirens began to wail. She stood in shadows near a trail leading into the woods beside the lake after which the town was named.

The precinct faced the blue waters of the lake, and the trees shivered as she gasped, trying to regain her breath, adrenaline pumping, folders clutched desperately in hand.

She took a few steps into the dark path under the trees—a jogger's path—and approached an old, ancient stump of a tree that had been in Pinelake longer than she ever had.

She collapsed onto the stump, panting and sweating, but relieved to be alive.

As she sat there, trying to catch her breath, she couldn't help but wonder what had possessed her to think *any* of this was a good idea.

Now, though, hands trembling, she glanced down at the folders she'd taken. She set these on the edge of the stump. Small etchings and carvings ornamented the wood, displaying where vandals had come through, leaving their mark.

She then pulled the dopp kit from where she'd slipped it into her waistband, leaving it next to the folders.

Still breathing slowly, she stared at the items, her brow furrowed deeply. For one long moment, she just sat there, staring. The sirens continued in the distance but now sounded as if they were heading in the other direction.

She couldn't linger long. The FBI was on her case as well.

Thinking of the FBI made her think of Agent Forester. The tall ex-boxer and self-proclaimed sociopath had helped her initially. Now, she didn't know what had happened to him.

The last she'd heard had been gunshots from the house where he'd stayed behind, allowing her to escape.

Thinking about it, though, only made her more uncomfortable. Thinking of Forester often had this effect. The man was *not* a safe person. But he'd been there . . . and now, alone, isolated, she felt small and scared.

"I play a game for a living," she muttered out loud, as if somehow, *speaking* the words would help it make more sense.

She wasn't an agent. For years, she'd spent most of her life in her apartment, *avoiding* others and attempting to keep her life as insulated as possible.

And now. . .

The siren continued to wail behind her. Her shoulders shook as she stared at the evidence on the stump. Two folders, a dopp kit. All of it considered important enough to be left inside a safe.

She shivered again and closed her eyes.

She could feel tears welling up.

If only to avoid this further embarrassment, she reached out, snatching at the dopp kit and opening it in one quick motion.

The zipping sound accompanied her opening eyes. And she stared into the kit, breathing slowly.

CHAPTER 12

She reached in, hesitantly, and her fingers found the same cold item she'd felt before. It took her a second to realize it was an old plastic cord. A black cord—like the type found jutting out of any number of television sets or computers nowadays.

But the cord was wrapped a few times with twine.

That was it.

A dopp kit and cord.

She stared at the item briefly, wrinkling her nose.

The Ghost-killer had targeted at *least* seven women. The number was still disputed. But all seven young women, mostly in their late teens or early twenties, had been killed by strangulation.

Even as she thought this, Artemis grimaced and slowly lowered the cord, realizing—perhaps—that she was holding the murder weapon.

Helen had left Tommy a note. Helen had said she'd been investigating.

And now Helen was missing.

"One step at a time," Artemis muttered to herself. It was all becoming too much. She got to her feet slowly, gripping the cord tight. She held it up, as if somehow the moonlight through the trees might aid interpretation.

But as she lifted it, as she held it aloft, the cold touch of the cord against her fingers added nothing further.

Had her father used this to kill those women?

Artemis stared at the cord, then glanced back inside the kit. She noticed a small, laminated note—like the type found dangling from a corpse's toe. She reached in, pulling out the note, trying not to think too morbid of thoughts, and then she read it carefully.

Murder weapon. Case number pending. Victim name pending. Suspect name: Otto Blythe.

She frowned now. Holding the small note in one hand and the supposed murder weapon in the other. Her father had used a cable to strangle these women. She dropped the cable, allowing it to fall back against the dopp kit, sending one of the dangling zippers swaying on the miniature cloth case.

Having lowered the murder weapon, she reached for the two folders now. She opened one and realized it was a printout of every victim's name, face, and history.

She winced as she scanned from one victim to the next, trying not to read their names or look at their faces. She'd seen occasional glimpses in the media before. It was nearly impossible not to. But now, as she scanned the faces of each printed, black-and-white photo on the paper files, she couldn't help but notice things.

Bronze curls. Smiling eyes. In the victim history section, she spotted academic accolades. Intelligent young women.

All of them exactly as Artemis had been told. Each of them looking very much like Helen Blythe. Each of them like Artemis' sister.

Seven of them. The first had been killed three years before her father had ever been caught. Artemis would've only been seven years old at the time. The next one had been killed the same year. She didn't study the names. She didn't want to know.

But the faces were harder to avoid. It felt as if the faces were staring at her, watching, accusing. She shivered as she flipped to the second folder.

The information had been scant in the first one. Victim history didn't help her nearly as much. All of the victims had lived in Pinelake or the surrounding area. All of them had been local. All of them had shared the same features and profile.

One of the victims in particular, though, caught Artemis' attention.

She'd been in the middle of closing the file and reaching for the second folder when she spotted the final victim.

A woman by the name of Roberta Green.

Nineteen years old. A recent college graduate, having started school at the age of sixteen. She'd been preparing to go into a master's degree.

The reason Ms. Green's name had caught Artemis' attention was because the face was one she *particularly* recognized. How could she not? *This* was the victim who'd been found dead in the Ghost-killer's bed with him.

Video footage from Otto's own security system had shown him with his arm wrapped around the dead woman, holding her close as if snuggling with the corpse.

Artemis grimaced, trying to push the images from her mind.

But one of the drawbacks of having such a clear memory was that it proved difficult to dismiss such thoughts when they came knocking. Now, she sat there on the stump, one hand bunched in her lap, glaring in frustration at the photo of the woman.

She, if anything, looked the *least* like Helen.

The hair color, for one, was wrong. In the right light, it might have looked *orange* rather than bronze. This young woman also wasn't nearly as pretty as Helen had been once upon a time. Most of the other victims had been young and attractive.

But there was something in the eyes of the old picture.

Roberta Green had intelligent eyes. This, though, would've been obvious anyway. Now, Artemis released a slow, rattling breath, shaking her head and muttering to herself as she leaned back, arms crossed over her chest.

Roberta Green had been found dead in Otto's bed.

As she opened the second folder, now, closing the first if only to block out the accusing glare in Ms. Green's gaze, Artemis read the heading.

She sat alone under the trees, inhaling the scent of the lake, listening to the now-quiet night. She frowned as she read the heading of the second folder again.

Final Deposition. Victim no.7. RG.

Artemis hesitated, wrinkling her nose, and she hastily scanned through this second folder's file. A printout of a transcript by the look of things. A transcript concerning Roberta Green's murder.

This, she realized, had been the nail in the coffin. The slam dunk the DA had used to prosecute Otto Blythe.

The oldest victim of the Ghost-killer had been Sheriff Dawkins' first wife—only twenty-nine at the time. His youngest victim had been Roberta Green at nineteen.

This the DA had emphasized during the interrogation. The transcript of the interview pulled no punches. The accusations against Otto flew fast.

Artemis read, frowning, murmuring under her breath as she landed on a particular section of the deposition.

DA: We know what you did, Otto. There's no use playing games now.

O: I still don't know what you mean, John.

DA: You killed her. You saw the footage.

O: That's not me.

DA: It is you. That's your bed, that's you.

O: Someone must've tampered with it, John. I never hurt so much as a fly.

DA: You lie for a living, Otto. I only wish I'd seen it sooner, you asshole. We found the murder weapon, by the way. A cable—under your bed. Is that what you used with all your victims?

O: I don't have victims, John.

DA: Why do you keep doing that?

O: Doing what?

DA: Repeating my name like that? Is that one of your mentalist tricks?

The transcript continued like this for a while longer, but now as Artemis read it, she wrinkled her nose, reading it once more. The majority of the case, it seemed, came down to finding Ms. Green dead in her father's bed. Strangled like the others.

Evidence following that had been accumulated. Travel patterns of Otto. Fingerprints on the cable under the bed. A few other items.

But the only *slam dunk* portion of the case had been the dead woman in the murderer's bed.

And now, Artemis was feeling a slow frown crease her features.

She hadn't wanted to look at any of it before. Not *really*. She'd known her father had done it. Everyone had known. Why rehash what was fact?

So she hadn't looked closely.

But now. . .

Now she was looking very closely, and something wasn't adding up.

Her father was a manipulator and a liar. She'd always known that. But he wasn't an imbecile. The murder weapon *with his fingerprints* had been found under the bed. The body of his latest victim had been found *in* his bed. And the security camera in his own house had been facing the bed.

There was only one problem. . .

This all made her father out to be an idiot.

Which he wasn't.

"No, no, no," she breathed slowly, her breath fogging. She pushed to her feet, frowning and shooting a look over her shoulder, but then moving once more down the jogger's path. She held the kit and the folders under one arm.

With her free hand she pulled her phone from her pocket and placed a call. Something wasn't adding up.

And she knew just the person to clarify it.

CHAPTER 13

"When you would steal money from the tin over Dad's dresser, re-member?"

A pause. Tommy cleared his throat. Artemis felt her impatience rising. She was still moving around the path near the lake, keeping to the dark trails, to the trees. She was breathing heavier now, and under the night sky, she could feel time running out.

Only five hours left until she was due to meet with Fake-Helen and exchange prisoners.

Her mind flitted to Jamie Kramer, to his sister Sophie, but she shook her head, forcing herself to focus, keeping her phone pressed to her cheek.

"Say that again," her brother replied. "You're breaking up—where are you?"

"Don't worry about that," she said, breathing slowly, standing at the base of an old willow tree, the branches above curling around her, creating a drooping umbrella as if shielding her from sight. The scent of the lake had diminished somewhat. The night had fallen thick and fast.

She was further in the forest preserve surrounding Pinelake, and could just about, through the wavering branches, spot the mountain range up near Leavenworth—the tall peaks standing out like shadows on the skyline.

"When you were a kid," she said. "You used to snatch change from Dad's dresser."

"Allegedly," he shot back.

"Drop gangster mode for a moment. This is important."

"Alright. Important. And?"

"The camera Dad had in his room," she replied. "The one he kept facing the back patio door—"

"I remember it, what about it?"

"Did he ever face it toward the bed?"

"What? Yuck."

"No—don't be weird. This is crucial," she said, breathing heavily now and tapping a foot against the ground. "Did dad ever face the camera toward his bed."

"Not that I know of, why would he?"

"So when you stole the change, you never moved it?"

"No."

"Like *never*?" she said.

Tommy paused for a moment, and she could practically see her brother's mismatched eyes narrowing in irritation. He said, "Never."

She let out a shaking breath, nodding to herself as she did. "That's what I thought."

"Why? How's that important?"

"Dad's not an idiot."

Tommy paused. Artemis adjusted her posture, her back scraping against the rough bark of the old willow tree. The ground was soft underfoot, and the whistle of the breeze through the long, dangling branches lifted the foliage and sent it fluttering like a trailing skirt.

"I mean," Tommy said, "depends who you ask."

"He's an asshole," she shot back. "But not a moron. He's smart."

"Yeah, so?"

"So. . ." She swallowed. "Why was the murder weapon under his bed?"

"How's that?"

"They found the murder weapon under his bed, with his prints on it."

"I mean. . ." Tommy coughed delicately. "Maybe he never thought anyone would look there. He'd gotten away with it for a while. I mean . . . Dad's always been a bit of a narcissist."

"I thought you believed he was innocent," she said, moving again now and brushing from under the willow tree. The branches trailed against her, tickling against her cheek, her arm. She picked up the pace, moving toward the third parking lot in the preserve. She glanced at her phone's screen, checking the notifications. The taxi was on the way.

She bit her lip, moving faster, kicking up dust on the trail, glancing off to her side and spotting the lunar reflection of blue light across the docile lake.

"I think it's possible," Tommy replied. "Helen said so, sis."

"Right. . ."

"You believe me?" he shot back.

"Yes!" Artemis retorted. "It had to have been Helen. I've been playing the annotation out in my head. It's *exactly* the game we played."

"The chess notes?"

"Yeah. The paper is annotation of our chess match. Only the three of us were in that boat. You were fishing, facing the other way. Only Helen and I could've *possibly* memorized that game. The odds of anyone else guessing it are less likely than the odds of a star to randomly implode. It's impossible."

"Don't know much about imploding stars," Tommy said conversationally. "But hang on a second . . . so the game matches?"

"Yeah. Exactly." Artemis nodded, moving quickly, arms swinging at her sides, face caught by the cool breeze. Time was running out. Only five hours left. Five hours until Fake-Helen would want to meet.

And Artemis was no closer to solving this thing. To figuring out *what* was going on. Who Fake-Helen was. If her father was actually involved or not.

One step at a time.

She strode forward.

One step at a time. . .

She said, "It's the exact same. She even annotates the draw I offered and the draw declined."

"So it has to be Helen. So . . . Helen *has to be alive*!" Tommy exclaimed suddenly, and for a brief moment, he didn't sound like a jaded, cynical man who'd been kicked around by life. Rather, his voice rose in excitement, and she could hear the delight in his tone.

"She has to be. At least when you met her," Artemis shot back. "*After* she disappeared. A year *after* I left Pinelake . . . so. . ." She frowned.

"Three years after Helen disappeared," Tommy said, still sounding giddy. "She's alive. She was alive when she was eighteen, then."

"Yeah . . . yeah I guess so."

"So where is she?"

Artemis bit her lip. She didn't want to voice her great fear. But part of her wondered if the Ghost-killer had caught up with Helen. What if he'd killed her while she'd been investigating the crimes her father had been accused of?

Artemis frowned, shaking her head, realizing for a second, as her mind churned, that this line of thought lent itself to one conclusion.

The innocence of Otto Blythe.

"Shit. . ." she muttered under her breath.

"What?"

"Just. . ."

"Dad?"

"Yeah," she said slowly.

Neither of them spoke for a moment. Artemis was still breathing quickly as she marched up the worn road. She had a skip to her step as she hastened forward. Her brow was furrowed deeply, and she felt her phone suddenly buzz, alerting her that the taxi had arrived in the eastern parking lot of the preserve.

She took a left turn on the trail, still moving fast.

"If Dad's innocent," she said slowly. "Then . . . shit. I've been an ass to him. He's been serving nearly two decades for something he didn't do."

"Yeah. Yeah, I've thought about that," her brother said quietly.

Neither of them said anything. Neither of them had *anything* they could say. They couldn't make it right. They couldn't make themselves feel better. Artemis had thought her father was a monster, had believed every charge against him.

Now. . .

Having been falsely accused herself, she thought of Agent Forester. He'd believed her. She thought of Dr. Bryant—the coroner had *also* believed her.

How come she hadn't ever believed her own father?

"Dad was a liar," she said quietly. "A manipulator. He conned people out of money for a living."

Tommy just grunted.

He didn't disagree. They both knew what she was saying was true. Their father *had* been an untrustworthy man. Had been a liar and a manipulator and a deceiver.

And yet. . .

That didn't mean he was a killer.

But this, she supposed, was partly *why* she hadn't believed him when he'd protested his innocence. Her father wasn't just the boy who'd cried wolf. He was the boy who'd screamed wolf through a megaphone ten thousand times.

And yet, she still couldn't shake the guilt.

"I mean. . . Just because it was dumb to leave the camera facing the bed. . . Maybe he *wanted* to be caught," she said quickly.

"Do you believe that?"

"No. No, I don't."

"So someone framed him," Tommy said simply.

She bit her lip, nodding. "Yeah . . . someone did. But who?"

"I mean . . . a *lot* of people were screwed out of money with Dad's con," Tommy said slowly. "Maybe that's a good place to start."

"Yes!" Artemis exclaimed. "You're right—*yes*. But how. . ." She trailed off, her mind thinking. Her father had pretended to be a psychic for years. He would often perform shows, happily taking money while lying through his teeth to the audience.

Other times, he'd performed mentalism, not quite claiming to be psychic but happily implying it. All of the shows had taken place in Pinelake. Had been done through a small stage that was also used for the local theater and the occasional musician that came through.

"Is *Plato Theater* still owned by Amy Doncic?" she said quickly.

"Umm . . . lemme check." A pause. Then her brother said, "Yeah. Looks like Jasper, her boy, helps too. But Amy's still the owner."

"What's her address?"

"Shit—you gonna talk to her *now*?"

"I need that information, Tommy. I need to know who might have complained about Dad. Might've threatened him. He wouldn't have been reachable. But the one who booked him on the stage—the venue owner?"

"Huh . . . yeah, fair," said Tommy. "Alright, hang on, I'm sending you her address. Just . . . you know. Careful, Art."

"Yeah, you too."

And she hung up, hastening toward the taxi, which she now spotted through the trees, headlights glowing, and gripping her phone tightly as she waited for the address from her brother.

If someone had framed her father, then it would've been someone who'd *wanted* him to spend his life behind bars.

Someone who'd wanted him to suffer.

And the people whose emotions he'd played with, the people he'd tricked into giving him money—these would be the most likely suspects.

Would Ms. Doncic still have access to records from twenty years ago?

It was a long shot.

But Artemis didn't have anywhere else to turn.

And time was still ticking.

She broke into a jog, waving her phone above her head, signaling at where the taxi idled.

CHAPTER 14

The door to the yellow cab shut behind her with a *thud*. She frowned up in the direction of the small house set on the cliff, overlooking the valley below.

She tugged at her sleeves and adjusted her hair, brushing it behind her pale ears. She nibbled her lip hesitantly, standing in the dark and glancing at her phone again.

Only four hours until her rendezvous for the prisoner exchange.

She shook her head, moving hastily up the path leading to the top of the cliff and trying to calm her nerves as she approached the hundred-year-old house overlooking the valley.

No lights.

No movement.

A couple of trucks were parked in front of an old, three-car garage. As Artemis approached the dusty driveway, her phone in front of her illuminating the ground, she could hear an animal inside the house begin to bark and yip.

She winced as the dog made enough racket to wake the dead and nearly paused to turn back.

But the desperation of the moment forced her forward. There was no turning back now. She'd come this far, and she had to go further.

She found her breath coming quickly, her heart pounding, and she reached the large pink door with peeling paint. She reached out a hand, hesitantly.

The dog was still barking.

She wasn't sure exactly *how* to broach the topic. Even having had time to rehearse in the car. Her hair was tied back now, and she was—of all things—wearing sunglasses on her head.

It was dark, but she needed *something* to help hide her appearance.

Now, as she braced to knock on the door, she reached up, lowering the sunglasses. Her hair in a ponytail, her eyes concealed, she hoped it was enough to disguise her identity at least long enough to get what she needed.

That was . . . as long as Mrs. Doncic didn't just *instantly* call the cops on someone waking her from her sleep at two A.M.

Artemis winced, knocked twice. The dog seemed to bark in rhythm with the blows. And then a light turned on above her from the second floor, the glow extending out in the darkness.

Artemis felt a flicker of unease. At any moment, she could turn back and hide. She glanced down the trail she'd taken, toward where she could just barely spot the glow of the taxi's brake lights on the asphalt.

But again, she steeled herself.

The niggling uncertainty from earlier was returning now with a vengeance.

Her father might be innocent. *Might.*

He wasn't a stupid man. And her brother's testimony had proven what she'd been fearful of. The camera in her father's bedroom had been purchased out of *fear* during a slew of break-ins when she'd been only five. The break-ins had occurred in their neighborhood—someone was stealing from the homes in the area.

And so, her father had purchased the camera for *his* room, since the glass door led from his bedroom to the patio.

But the camera had *always* faced the patio. So why would it ever have pointed at the bed, unless someone had intentionally turned it?

The corpse in the bed?

No. . . No, someone had put her father on the line. She was beginning to believe it more and more. If Helen thought their dad was innocent, and if Tommy was now going along with it, how could she deny it?

But she wouldn't commit to believing it. Not yet.

How could she?

Too much was riding on it.

Artemis shivered slowly, arms wrapped around her body, waiting on the porch, facing the large door.

And then she heard the sound of creaking footsteps against wood. A low voice, the sound of muttered pleadings. The barking dog refused to listen to its master's placations and continued merrily yipping into the night.

And then, Artemis heard a voice through the door.

"Who is it?"

Those words were like a spotlight, highlighting her where she stood. Her hands jammed into her pockets, and she trembled. She was still wearing those glasses, her hair brushed back. And then, glancing down, then up again, she realized that although she was wearing sweatpants and a sweater, she *was* clad in all black. Her shoes were black.

Her sunglasses black.

And so, she sighed. "Special Agent Shauna Grant, FBI!" she called out, her voice cracking at first, but then she recovered.

She cleared her throat as she called.

A pause.

Artemis' could *hear* her own heartbeat. *Thump. Thump. Thump-thump.* It skipped a beat.

And then, the voice said, "Who?"

"FBI!" she called even more forcefully, using her time with Agent Desmond Wade and Cameron Forester to channel all the authority and confidence those two agents employed when in the field.

The last thing she currently felt was confidence, but she could play the part. At least for a moment.

She was here for information. And she had only a few hours left until she was meant to meet up with Fake-Helen.

Until she found out the truth about the Ghost-killer, she was no closer to discovering if her father was really innocent, if Fake-Helen was playing some *other* game here, or if this was all just farce.

So she stood her ground, arms crossed, doing her best to keep an appearance of confidence.

After a moment, the door slowly opened, creaking on the hinges as it did. A bright blue eye behind the left frame of horn-rimmed glasses peered out into the night.

Artemis stood there, arms still crossed, peering from behind her sunglasses. She knew her appearance didn't exactly scream *professional*. But she had two things going for her. First, the disoriented state of the woman. Late at night, in the dark, with Mrs. Doncic currently sleep deprived, Artemis' best tactic was not to hesitate.

Not to give the woman a chance to think through the claims.

Would an FBI agent really show up this late at night? Where was the badge? Would an FBI agent *look* like this, wearing sweatpants and a sweater?

All these questions were death knells.

The second advantage Artemis had—whether considered fair or not—was that she was a woman. And to *another* woman, late at night, a small, petite woman wearing sweatpants and with nothing in her hands that might be seen as threatening, Artemis would seem far less of a threat than if she'd been a man.

And so, she moved and spoke quickly. She didn't step forward but rather back for two reasons. First, she needed the shadows. The door was illuminating the porch now, and Artemis wanted to hide herself before it was too late.

Secondly, she didn't want to alarm the old theater owner.

Mrs. Doncic, for her part, opened the door a bit further as Artemis re-treated, perhaps out of a sense of more comfort now that the stranger was further back, or perhaps to get a better look and allow more light to wash the porch.

The old woman had curling, silver hair. . . Though after a few seconds, Artemis supposed it was a wig, judging by how it sat skewed on the older woman's head.

She wore horn-rimmed glasses, and her bright blue eyes peered out from behind the frames. The woman was also hunched and leaning over, a small puppy cradled in her arms. A wizened hand scooped up the front legs of the small hound, holding its chest and keeping it from darting toward Artemis.

The small dog was panting rapidly, a tiny pink tongue prodding out from its lips. Artemis didn't know much about dogs, but this particular one looked like a Chihuahua.

Now, the dog's bugged, black eyes were staring directly at Artemis, and a low growl crept into the creature's voice.

But Artemis spoke quickly, riding over the hound's protests. She didn't have time; she knew that much. "Mrs. Doncic?" she said quickly, remembering everything that her brother had read to her. "Your son is Jasper Doncic?"

The woman in the door was still peering out from behind her glasses, wearing a sleek, pale nightgown with miniature pink bows along the sleeves and chest. Now, the woman blinked again, and a note of concern crossed her expression.

"I'm sorry, what did you say your name was again?"

"Agent Shauna Grant," Artemis said firmly. "I'm sorry about the late hour of the visit, but as I'm sure you know from the news cycle, we've had some goings-on recently in Pinelake."

The woman wrinkled her nose. "I don't watch the news." She yawned, holding a hand up to her lips. She glanced at Artemis' sunglasses, then her eyes moved, trailing along Artemis' sweatpants and sweater. She looked suspicious now, and her eyes narrowed behind her glasses.

Artemis, who'd always been a student of human nature and body language, could feel her heartbeat quickening.

The last thing she needed was for Mrs. Doncic to slam the door and call the cops. Artemis had stepped back to provide distance and a sense of safety, but now the woman was using this full-length view to give Artemis a once-over.

Artemis said hurriedly, "Your son, Jasper, is he home?"

It was a dirty trick. But the best way to replace suspicion or critical thinking was to arouse fear. It was the same reason that a small niggle in the throat one night might seem like a life-threatening medical condition the *next* night. The only difference might have been an online article or a throwaway comment by a friend.

It was fear. Fear could make morons of the brightest minds. Fear would make fools of the wisest sage if given too much purchase.

Artemis didn't *want* to scare this woman, but she also couldn't retreat. And so, she said, "Is Jasper here, ma'am?"

"I . . . yes. . ." the woman said, eyes still narrowing suspiciously.

Artemis glanced at the two trucks in the driveway. One likely belonged to the woman's son and the other to Mrs. Doncic herself.

But by making this an issue concerning the woman's *son*, Artemis hoped to keep her on the back heel.

"Where's your badge—" Doncic began.

But Artemis cut in before the woman could finish. "Was your son working with you at *Plato Theater* when the Ghost-killer was working for you?"

She said it blunt, cold and direct.

Again, the combination of knowledge—how else would she have known about the Ghost-killer's connection to the theater if she *wasn't* an FBI agent—and also the sheer confidence was enough to provide some emotional credibility.

And again, before Doncic could protest, Artemis said, "Was he? Jasper was how old at the time, ma'am?"

"Jasper was . . . what is this about?"

"Your theater, *Plato's Theater*," Artemis insisted. "That's what it is called, yes?"

"Y-yes . . . but. . ." The woman wrinkled her nose. "Is Jasper in trouble?"

Finally, her sleep-deprived mind was making connections. And thankfully, these were the connections Artemis wanted her to make. Focus on the son, not on the woman in the stupid glasses on the porch.

And again, Artemis blitzed. She couldn't give time for thinking. Couldn't hesitate.

"We have reason to believe that someone is targeting friends of the Ghost-killer," Artemis said quickly. "Otto Blythe used to rent your theater, Mrs. Doncic. Jasper might be involved."

This last part was a complete fabrication, but again, Artemis needed to keep the fear stoked and to keep Doncic engaged. Even as she said it, though, she felt her stomach twist in guilt. She did *not* enjoy all of this business of living outside the law.

The lying, the manipulation, even for a good cause—it made her stomach turn.

"Jasper was only eight at the time!" Doncic snapped. "Who have you been talking to? Is it Randy? It's Randy, isn't it! I told him I'd sue—we have a restraining order!"

Artemis paused only briefly. She cycled through the potential options of who this *Randy* character might be. Further credibility could only help her case now.

As she considered the anger in Doncic's voice and the *immediate* connection, Artemis wondered if perhaps *Randy* was a business rival or a lover. The two seemed the most likely explanations. A restraining order was often taken against personal connections. But the claim of *I'd sue!* suggested a more civil concern.

Artemis guessed but left herself a backdoor in case she was wrong. "You have a personal connection with Randy, right? A business issue." Personal. And business. Vague enough to allow deniability. But specific enough to suggest credibility.

A mentalist's best weapon, in her father's estimation, was always the mind of their target.

Now, though, this new display of knowledge earned Artemis even more credibility. The woman with the pale curls was bobbing her head and tsking her tongue, muttering, "He thinks that if he runs down my business, he'll get my clients. But he doesn't have the track record I do!"

"Of course not," Artemis said quickly, easily taking on the role of comforter.

From fear to comfort. An easy way to use someone's emotions against them. It was an age-old trick. Hire someone to mug a person in an ally, then show up just in time to save them, thus ingratiating one's self into the good graces of the target.

This was the emotional version of it.

And now, Artemis stepped forward. "We were concerned it might have been something like that," Artemis said, wishing that the lie hadn't tumbled so easily off her tongue. She forced herself to focus on Jamie, though. On Sophie. Forced her mind to stick to the motive behind all of it.

"I'll make sure we don't let him get away with false testimony," she said. "But I need you to answer some questions. On the porch is fine, if you'd prefer. Again, I apologize for the late visit."

The more Artemis spoke in comforting tones and the more she apologized, the more at ease Doncic seemed to appear. The dog in her arms, though, was still growling.

Artemis continued, still keeping up the rapid pace. "We need to know of anyone who made threats to Otto Blythe. Do you keep records of customer complaints? Customer service reports? Anything like that?"

The woman hesitated, pausing only briefly. "Otto Blythe... Of course I remember him, but that was . . . twenty years ago!" she protested. "I don't keep anything *that* long."

Artemis' heart sunk, but she didn't relent. She'd come here for information. This was an obstacle, *not* a dead end. Not yet.

She said, "You're not in trouble, Mrs. Doncic. But if there's anything you can remember, it would prove invaluable to me and my field office."

The older woman shook her head, trying to stroke the ears of the growling mutt in her hand. She paused, considering the options, and then said, "I don't know what you want from me. There's nothing I've seen. It was *so* long ago. What does Jasper have to do with this again?"

Artemis said, "Maybe nothing. But the more information I have, the more I can clear this up. Was there anyone that contacted you, threatening you or the theater?"

"I'm sure we've had threats occasionally. Some drunken brawls. But nothing unusual."

Artemis hesitated. She realized that the woman was currently in reputation protection mode. Artemis needed to get the woman to open up. So she said, "You threatened legal action against this Randy, didn't you?"

"Yes. . ."

"And it was over business disputes?" Again, more guesswork but easy guesswork.

The woman frowned, still looking suspicious. But now, it seemed as if the suspicion was directed more toward the intention behind Artemis' words, rather than the identity of the woman in front of her. Again, the sleep, the dark, all of it was playing to Artemis' advantage. She played it well. But now, it wouldn't matter if she didn't get the information she needed. She needed something, a lead.

This was a woman who had proven that she could be litigious if needed. And so, Artemis said, "Did you ever contact the police, threatening a lawsuit against anyone who made threats against *Plato's Theater*?"

"It was so long ago. . ."

"Specifically concerning Otto Blythe," Artemis said quietly.

And as she said her father's name, she spotted something flicker in the old woman's eyes.

One moment, Doncic opened her mouth to protest completely, but the next, her jaw closed again. Her lips pressed in a small, thin line. She swallowed and looked away. The dog was still growling in her arms.

She paused only briefly and then said, "Well, I of course didn't invite him back after the charges were pressed."

"I'm more concerned about anything before that. Any customer, a paying customer, who came to you? Who complained?"

"Not a customer, no. . ."

Bingo. Something in the voice. The woman had remembered something. Artemis could see it in the flicker of her eyes. The hesitation. And so, Artemis pointed, nodding once, her head bobbing in the shadows. The dog was still growling, but Artemis ignored it, and instead, she said, "*That*. Whatever you just considered. What is it?"

The woman paused. She gave a hesitant shake of her head. She looked away, as if considering things, but then looked back and said, "I'm sure it's nothing, but. . ." She frowned into the night and said, "it was very long ago."

"That's fine."

"But Randy," she said suddenly, meeting Artemis' gaze and holding it. "Randy Cortez. He runs the dance Academy in Eaglewood. We've always had issues with each other. Mostly on his end, of course. He

wanted to buy that theater, before I managed to get it . . . but . . . but.
. ." She paused, blinking a few times and staring off. "I do remember
an issue *his* daughter had with Otto."

"And you remember Otto?"

The woman snorted. "Agent Grant, *everyone* in this town remembers
Otto Blythe. That psychopath's kids were in the same school as my
Jasper—poor dears. . ." she said softly, sighing. "Some blame the kids,
but that's heartless if you ask me."

Artemis didn't react to this, but she felt a wave of fondness for the older
woman wash over her. Instead, she said, speaking hurriedly, "So what
did Mr. Cortez do that makes you connect him to my question?"

"Oh . . . it was what . . . twenty years? That's what you said, right?"
The old woman nodded shrewdly. "Randy is a bastard. Hear me? A
bastard!" She lifted one of her puppy's drooping ears and spoke into it,
as if announcing the term to the hound. She snickered, then glanced at
Artemis and cleared her throat. "Er, I mean to say, he was also a crook.
Ties to the mob, actually."

Artemis didn't blink at this. "Oh?"

"Yes. Yes, and I had business disputes with him. But I remember this
time when he threatened to take away my best client. It was Otto at the
time. He was performing three shows a week and paying better than
ten other clients combined."

Artemis hesitated. "So. . . Randy threatened you?"

147

"No—well, yes. But he threatened to poach my client. He said he would offer Otto a better deal."

"And then?"

"He couldn't. Otto Blythe wanted the space that my theater offered." She shrugged sheepishly and scratched at a wart on the side of her face absentmindedly. Her eyes crinkled in the corners. "And so, he got angry. Said he'd make us both pay."

"He said that?" Artemis asked.

"Well, not in so many words. He said something like, *we'll see about that*, once I told him he'd failed. Otto was sticking with Plato's." She waved a hand and sniffed. "Really, I don't remember it that well. So what has Randy been saying, then?"

But Artemis paused. "Is there anyone else you can think of? Anyone else who wanted to cause trouble?"

"Not that comes to mind. Otto was good at protecting himself. He never released personal information publicly. No . . . no, the only time he ever allowed business and his private life to mix was when he took the meeting with Cortez at his home."

Artemis held out her hands suddenly, like a traffic warden attempting to stop an oncoming bus. "Hang on," she said urgently. "You're saying that this Cortez fellow *knew* where Otto lived?"

"Yes. He must've. The two of them had lunch. Is that relevant?"

But Artemis was turning now. She could feel prickles erupting along her skin. She picked up her pace, moving away and calling out, "Thank you, Mrs. Doncic. I need to be off!"

"What did you say your name was again?" the woman called. The suspicion had returned to her voice.

But Artemis didn't stop. Didn't look back. She jammed her hands into her pockets and moved quickly.

Otto had been visited by Randy Cortez. Randy Cortez had threatened to *end* Mrs. Doncic's career by poaching Otto. But Otto had refused.

And Cortez had mob connections.

What if *he* was the Ghost-killer and had used the body in Otto's bed to kill two birds with one stone? To get the cops off his own trail while also imprisoning his rival's best client. . .

It was possible.

And if Cortez had mob connections, she could think of at least one person who might know how to find him.

CHAPTER 15

Artemis listened to the low grumble of a motorcycle engine. She stood at the gas station where the two of them had agreed to meet, under the cover, loitering near the bathrooms if only to keep herself hidden from the occasional motorist out and about this early in the morning.

Only three A.M. Time was quickly passing, and she had only a few hours left to meet up with Fake-Helen.

So many questions were still unanswered.

Was her father really the Ghost-killer?

If not, who was?

Had the Ghost-killer found Helen?

Was Artemis' sister *still* alive?

And how would they get the Kramers back if her father was innocent? The deal had been plain—Artemis had to turn in her father in exchange for Jamie, Sophie, and an alibi for Azin's murder. But now. . . If her father was innocent. . . Artemis couldn't just hand him over to a psychopath.

No. . . She needed conclusive evidence one way or another.

And that's why she stood out in the cold morning, her back to the glass window of the gas station. The building was empty. Only one motorist still lingered near a gas pump—an older man, puffing on a cigarette despite the warnings near the machine.

But her gaze turned in the direction of the approaching motorbike, and she watched as her brother arrived.

Tommy's long hair was loose now, fluttering behind him like a horse's mane. He was wearing his usual leather jacket and, to match the ones now in Artemis' pocket, sunglasses.

The two tattoos on the sides of his face stood out as he pulled into the gas station, kicked the kickstand, and hopped off his low-rider.

Tommy dusted his gloved hands off on one another, looked around, spotted her, and—in the dark of night—began to approach, sauntering forward as he drew near.

She watched as he approached, her heart pounding, her stomach twisted in knots.

She gave a quick nod and then, her voice low, she muttered, "Hey, thanks for meeting me."

"Yup," he said simply.

"So . . . where is he?"

Tommy jutted a thumb over his shoulder. "Cortez, you said, yeah?"

"Randy Cortez, yeah. Where?"

He nodded across the street now. "That's why we're meeting here, sis." He was looking toward the empty parking lot of a strip club. The neon sign out front read, *Heads and Tails.*

Artemis wrinkled her nose. "That's his business?"

"One of 'em. Also where he lives. Coupl'a nephews live with him, mind," Tommy said, a note of warning in his voice. He looked back at her, hands on his hips. "How come?" he said conversationally.

But Artemis was now peering toward the strip club across the street, frowning as she did. Was it possible that the Ghost-killer was the owner of local businesses in Pinelake and the surrounding area? Perhaps that was how he'd been able to avoid detection all these years.

As she considered it, she felt a jolt of frustration.

"I swore I'd never buy it," she said quietly, standing near her brother.

"Huh?" he said, clearly in a talkative mood.

"I told myself," she said simply, glancing at her brother now and meeting his shaded gaze, "that I'd *never* believe dad. Every time he said he was innocent, I knew he had an angle."

"Yeah, well . . . we all make mistakes."

"I just. . ." she swallowed. "Don't know which is the mistake. Believing him. Or not. Either way. . . It's all—"

"Screwed up. Yeah. Look, sis, don't worry about it. So you're thinking Cortez over there had something to do with it?"

"He knew where Dad lived and had reason to get Dad sent away for life. Plus . . . violent criminal."

Tommy snickered. "Oh, hell yeah. Cortez is as violent as they come."

She looked at her brother, frozen briefly. "R-really?"

"Yup. Once saw him shoot a man's kneecap off just for stealing his parking spot." Tommy combed his hair back with his fingers and then tied it with a scrunchy procured from his pocket. "Guess imma have to make introductions, huh?"

She shivered. "Really? You'd do that?"

"Shit, Artemis—why else would I drive out here? Come on, just, you know, don't say anything. Stick close. It'll be fine. Probably."

Her brother shrugged, snatched at her arm, and began guiding her across the asphalt, across the street, and toward the strip club.

As they moved, she could feel her stomach dropping and could feel a desperate desire to call the whole thing off.

What if Mrs. Doncic had simply used Artemis to go after Randy? What if she'd been set up?

This was the problem, Artemis decided, of working with such limited options, outside the box. She wasn't sure if she was being played.

She paced forward alongside her brother, heart in her throat, and wanting desperately to turn tail and run.

The two of them strode side by side, and Artemis felt a thin sweat break out across her forehead. Her hands felt clammy as they approached the front revolving door of the seedy strip club at three in the morning.

Confronting a gangster was hardly Artemis' definition of a good time.

But now, alongside her brother, she marched toward *Heads and Tails*. Together, the two of them likely cut an odd pairing. One, a woman with a nervous disposition and plain sweatpants. An unassuming figure who would only have been noted for her mismatched eyes had anyone gotten close enough to spot them.

The other, however, a tall, lanky man with sunglasses and wearing biker leathers. He had a saunter to his gait as if it was customary for him to march down dark streets, across abandoned parking lots to visit mobster hideouts.

He was even whistling softly under his breath as he strode forward.

The two of them brushed against each other, Artemis' shoulder against his bicep, as he was the taller of the two by a good margin.

As they approached, Tommy rattled off instructions under his breath. "Don't say anything about money. Oh, also don't mention that incident with the bikers."

"The-the what?"

"The bikers. The ones I blew up."

She shot him a quick look.

He shrugged back at her, his expression impassive. He added quickly, "Also, don't smile. Don't shake hands, and don't . . . say anything."

Artemis was frowning now. "That's a lot of don'ts," she murmured.

"Yeah, well. . . Don't pull out your phone either."

"Tommy . . . just how dangerous are these guys?"

"Bad," he said simply. "Real bad." He paused, shooting her a look, as the two of them had reached the glass doors of the strip club. He gave her a long look.

"What?" she said.

He replied, "I know Randy. His nephews are about as bad as he is. The three of them once found a rival family's employees alone at a junkyard. They put the guys in a car crusher."

Artemis winced.

"From what I hear, Randy enjoys that sorta thing. Straight-up sadist, I'm told."

"So . . . he might be the Ghost-killer?" she shot back.

"Huh. Maybe. But he's definitely not someone to screw around with. That clear?"

"Crystal." She could feel her nerves rising steadily.

The two of them had now come to a halt facing the rotating glass door of the strip club. Both of them scowled at the place, neither moving. Artemis waited for her brother to take the lead. Which he did by raising a hand, knocking on the door, and calling out.

"Hey, Cortez! Gotta chat."

Then he stepped back, his leather jacket swirling, turned on his heel, and bolted.

"Tommy!" she said sharply as her brother brushed past her, sprinting away from her and heading around the side of the building. "Tommy, where are you going!"

But her brother was running fast, and now he ducked around the side of the building, leaving Artemis standing like a doe caught in the headlights on the front steps, her mouth unhinged.

And then suddenly, two figures appeared in the rotating glass door. One of them was peering out at her, a scowl on his face, keys in hand. The keys could faintly be heard rattling on the other side of the glass as the man in question pushed the door open.

Both men had a unique look about them.

For one, they were twins.

For another, they were both albinos. Each of them with pale hair and pinkish eyes. Their skin was sallow and frail like thin parchment on the verge of being punctured. They each wore a neat, tidy, and expensive-looking suit.

Both men's prematurely pale hair was cut short and combed to the side like a choir boy's. They each wore tasteful golden skeleton watches visible just past the hems of their sleeves, and they were both peering out into the night at her, scowls etched across their matching features.

She wouldn't have described either of them as particularly handsome. But they were *fit*. Athletic and strong, judging by the way they carried themselves and the muscles apparent in their motions.

Now, both of their hands trailed near their thighs, resting against what appeared to be weapons holstered just under their suit jackets' hems.

Neither of them spoke at first but glanced at her from where they stood in the basin of the rotating door, then past her into the parking lot.

Artemis' knees were wobbly. She inwardly cursed Tommy, wondering where the hell her brother had gotten to.

Her gaze scanned the strip club, moving from the rotating door to the neon sign and a couple of tinted windows set ten or so feet off the ground.

Inwardly, she was a tangled mess of nerves.

But she forced a quick smile, nodding politely. Something told her that *this time* claiming to be a fed would only get her in trouble. These men didn't have a law-abiding look about them.

Besides, they weren't sleep deprived. If anything, they looked well-rested. Another somewhat irritating feature to go along with their fit, trim physiques.

Artemis, as so often the case when confronted by health nuts, vowed to start working out again.

But then her mind returned to the more proximate source of anxiety.

"I, er, hello," she said, swallowing faintly and waving a hand hesitantly. "I . . . I'm here to. . ."

She trailed off. She was never one for improvisation, though her blitz-game skills in fast-paced chess tournaments were some of her more lauded abilities.

Tommy had left her, slipping around the side of the club. And so, she improvised. She couldn't claim to be a fed, but. . .

Inwardly, she winced as the solution arrived. Vowing to kick Tommy in the shins if she got the chance to see him again—and that was looking like a big *if*, judging by the scowls on these men's faces—she cleared her throat and said, "I was hoping to apply for a job."

She flashed what she hoped was a winning smile and even stepped forward so that the light over the door could illuminate her mismatched but catching gaze.

"No jobs," snapped one of the men. His voice was high-pitched but cultured. The sort of voice that brought to mind images of estates and fast cars and hired accountants. Not at all Artemis' experience growing up in the foster system.

Now, though, she said hurriedly, "Are you sure?" She tried to smile again. "I would work for half pay. Is there someone I can speak to? Someone in charge?"

Both the men shared a look and then returned their attention to her. They eyed her up and down, but it was a dispassionate gaze and entirely predatory. Surprisingly, in their eyes, she didn't spot the sort of predatory look one might discover in the eyes of a man who worked at a strip club—the sort of gaze that spotted flesh instead of a person. Rather, it was a predatory look of a different variety.

The way someone might look at a bug on the sidewalk, as if deciding whether it was worth their trouble to step from their route in order to crush the thing.

An easy, quick crunch that offered some sort of satisfaction.

And now, both men took steps toward her, emerging from the rotating, glass doorway and eyeing her more attentively.

She shifted uncomfortably from one foot to the other and tried to force a quick smile. She even waved—though quickly dropped the hand as she realized how silly it looked.

"So. . ." said the man on the right who was indistinguishable from his brother. "Who are you here to speak with?"

A shrewd voice, a clever voice. And those pinkish eyes had narrowed suspiciously. The hand near the holster had gone rigid.

She hesitated, biting her lip, then shaking her head. "I. . ." She trailed off. They were here, of course, to investigate Mr. Cortez. But there was no easy way to say it without giving further suspicion.

Would a girl looking for a job off the street know the *name* of the establishment's proprietor?

According to her source, Mr. Cortez had wanted Otto Blythe in trouble. Would have benefited from framing her father for the murders. In addition, a mobster like Cortez might have been *exactly* the sort of person to prey on young women.

Glancing at the establishment's tawdry name, she couldn't help but make associations in her mind concerning the nature of a mobster who ran a place like this—specifically, the way in which he viewed women.

Pretty, young women. Just like Helen.

Just like the Ghost-killer's victims.

The more she dug, the more she began to fear that she'd been wrong about her father all these years. But the only absolution she could think of, the only apology she could offer, was the truth.

And so, instead of backing down, she redoubled her efforts. She leaned to the side, coughing delicately and trying to make her frame as small and nonthreatening as possible.

Granted, unarmed, wearing sweats, she didn't strike a particularly imposing figure to begin with.

"I can work cheap, and I have experience!" she said hurriedly. "I heard from a friend that you might be looking for new girls." She flashed a quick smile.

She'd always been told she was quite pretty. It was the reason she didn't wear makeup, didn't wear nice clothing. In her line of work, it was one thing to be excellent at chess—to be smarter than most of her online viewers.

But to be both smart *and* attractive. Neither men *nor* women liked it. Men felt threatened, women felt jealous. It took a rare person to allow both beauty and brains without having to tear the person down in their mind in order to make themselves feel better.

Artemis had felt a million times that she would've far, far rather have been plain and slow if it had meant she could have a family like the Kramers.

That was . . . until Mr. Kramer had gone psychotic and attacked his wife.

161

Either way, she'd always felt as if a family very much *unlike* hers would've been a greater advantage than the ones she'd been given.

But she supposed that was the nature of humanity, always looking for the greener grass.

The first twin who'd spoken initially opened his mouth, still scowling to protest, but before he could, his brother caught his shoulder, leaned in, and whispered something in the man's ear.

The twins both paused, carrying a quick, whispered conversation.

Then, the scowl on the first man's face faded faintly. He said, "Who told you we had jobs?"

She hesitated. "I . . . I'd rather not say until I speak to someone in charge."

"If you want to work here, you'll have to get used to the way things work."

"I still would rather speak to someone in charge."

The albino snorted, glared once more, and then moved *fast*. One moment he'd been standing with his back to the glass chamber of the rotating door, the next he darted forward, hand swinging and catching her across the face.

She yelped where his blow struck and reeled back. At the same time, though, he'd lashed out, catching her wrist and holding tight. He looked her dead in the eyes, glaring as he held her tight, like a mooring rope securing a vessel.

She hadn't realized just how strong the trim twin was but now could feel him putting all of his strength into his hand, squeezing so very tightly she thought something might crack.

She let out a hiss of pain, trying to withdraw her hand, but the albino said, quietly, in the dark of night—fully aware that there were no witnesses to watch them—"You'll need a more polite mouth on you, girl, if you want to work here." He squeezed tighter, eliciting a gasp of pain.

As she did, this almost seemed to arouse him. Watching a woman in pain, he seemed to breathe a bit heavier, his nostrils flaring, his blood pumping.

He shot a quick look back at his brother, and they both shrugged.

"She's pretty enough," said the first. "Uncle was saying we need more talent, you know how he is."

"Yeah. . . Yeah, I suppose so." The man holding her wrist shrugged again and then pulled her sharply before releasing.

She stumbled forward, fear flaring and lashing out with a hand to avoid colliding with the man. She pressed her fingers against his muscled chest, and he gave a low chuckle before turning slowly and gesturing. "You wanna speak to someone in charge, come on in then. Late night job interview," he said, shooting another look back at her, this time as if admiring her features.

Though it wasn't *quite* in the way one might glance at an attractive woman. Rather, it felt more like how someone might admire a particularly alluring sports car. Some *item.*

And feeling her heart skipping a beat, Artemis paused only briefly.

Only a few hours until Jamie Kramer and Sophie would need Artemis to show up at the rendezvous. Only a few hours until everything collapsed.

She couldn't linger.

She couldn't hesitate.

She still needed to find out what was going on. If her father was innocent. Who the real Ghost-killer was and how Fake-Helen was involved in all of it.

And so, she didn't step back.

Realizing it was a foolish choice but understanding also that Jamie was in far worse danger, she followed the two men through the rotating doors.

The glass swished around her, and she entered the strip club trembling faintly and wondering desperately what on earth Tommy was up to and where he'd gone.

CHAPTER 16

She sat in a luxurious office space, the red leather chair puffy from segments of foam, which swaddled her. The room smelled faintly of cherry blossoms, coming from the wood wick candle which sputtered on the desk.

Another candle was currently cradled in the hands of one of the twins, who was idling by the door, leaning in the door frame, and occasionally glancing in her direction.

The man lifted the candle, sniffed it faintly, then lowered it onto the table at his back. All the while, Artemis shifted uncomfortably, hands folded in her lap, eyes ahead.

The second twin had disappeared a few minutes ago, leaving her alone with her candle-sniffing chaperone.

The two of them hadn't spoken a word since entering the room, and now both of them maintained that silence. Artemis leaned back in the chair faintly, listening to it creak. At the same time, her eyes darted across the ornate desk in front of her.

The office in the strip club was a far more ornate affair than she'd initially anticipated.

There were pens sitting in a cup holder, each of them glinting gold. A small inkpot settled next to these pens. Over the fireplace and above the wood wick candle was a large, antlered head of an elk, stuffed. The marble, taxidermy eyes stared down at her, the long, branching horns casting eerie shadows due to the flame from the candle.

A fire was burning in the hearth *beneath* the candle, attempting to give the strip club office a more homey feel.

But it only made Artemis' skin crawl. Everything about her surroundings gave her more than a small amount of discomfort.

At least the man in the door hadn't come any closer.

But now, Artemis was running through options in her mind. She couldn't leave. That much was clear.

She'd come in order to speak with Cortez. But she was wondering exactly how she might *escape* once that happened. She was also still trying to figure out where Tommy had vanished to.

Had he gotten cold feet and fled?

That didn't sound like her brother, did it? He'd once broken her out of prison by ramming a car through a concrete wall. He'd climbed the side of a hospital to check on her.

No. . . No—Tommy was here *somewhere,* but she couldn't quite find where.

She looked over her shoulder toward a large oak bookshelf. Instead of books, though, there were stacks of magazines. By the looks of them, skin magazines, all of them arranged neatly and placed in plastic sleeves. The porn version of a comic book collection.

She looked away from the magazines, glancing back to the door.

The man there was watching her from beneath hooded eyes, his pinkish gaze fixating on her. Her skin crawled under his attention, and she looked away again.

But now, the man in the doorway spoke. "Quite pretty for a place like this," he said conversationally.

She didn't look at him.

"Hard troubles at home?" he said softly.

She still stared ahead.

"Or are you mostly interested in the money?"

She shrugged, nodding once but saying nothing.

He snickered. "Bitches like you always want the money, huh?"

She kept her attention on the fireplace. The man chuckled again. "You know, I dated a whore once. Bad mistake that."

Artemis paused but then swallowed faintly. At least he was in a chatty mood, and she'd come here for information, hadn't she? So she turned sharply in her chair, glancing at him. "Yeah? And how was that?" she said softly.

He smirked at the sudden shift in her attention and shrugged once. "Alright, I guess. At first. She knew her stuff, if you know what I mean." He wiggled his eyebrows. And again, he seemed to be breathing heavier. And again, it seemed directly proportional to the fear she was feeling.

Artemis opened her mouth to redirect the conversation, her hands clasped firmly in her lap, her back prickling.

But before she could interject, he continued, "Whore stole my car, though. Tried to poison me while I slept." He gave her a long look, his chuckle turning back to a scowl. "Are you a crazy bitch too?"

She didn't blink, didn't reply. It wasn't her job to correct the manners of every thug. Instead, she said, "Have you worked here long?"

He shifted and shrugged, puffing his chest importantly. "My uncle owns the place."

"Oh?" she said, trying to feign surprise as well as attempting to look impressed. "Wow. So you're kinda like an owner too, then, huh?"

He paused, and a look of worry crossed his face. He shot a quick look over his shoulder, as if searching for anyone else, but then, in a quiet tone, he said, "You might say that, yeah. You'll be answering to me if you get the job, mind."

She nodded. "Well. . . That's impressive. I've never owned anything like this."

He tapped his nose and pointed at her. "You'll like it soon enough. Good pay, good benefits." He winked.

She pretended as if her skin hadn't crawled and hid her look of disgust. Instead, she said, "So . . . it's been a while then. How long you've worked here, I mean. If your uncle owns the place. . ."

"Huh? Yeah, yeah. A few years. Me and my brother. That guy back there is the ugly twin," he said with a grin and a knowing wink, as if he was accustomed to eliciting laughs with this particular joke.

Artemis just frowned. She wanted to rise from the chair and look for something to defend herself with. The anxiety was the worst part. The unknown. It felt like bracing for a blow that one *knew* was coming but hadn't quite arrived yet.

Now, though, as she waited, she shot a look toward the fireplace again. She wasn't sure quite *how* to continue this conversation. She tried fluttering her eyelashes but didn't quite know which muscles to use. And so, instead, she attempted a vapid, playful voice. She'd never had much practice with flirting, though.

So in the end, she sighed and looked him dead in the eyes and said, "I know how to keep a secret, you know. I'm wanted for murder actually."

This last part came unbidden from her lips, and the moment she said it, she knew it was a gambit. A risky play.

But as the words registered, the man in the door looked impressed, his eyebrows rising. "Huh," he said. "That so? Where you wanted?"

She shook her head. "I'm just saying, I might be helpful in a place like *this.*"

He watched her, shrewdly now. "And what sort of place might that be?"

She shrugged. "Whatever."

He hesitated, scratched at his chin, then muttered, "Better bring that up with Uncle Cortez."

"Which part?"

"The murder part."

She winced. "Is . . . is that going to cost me the job?"

"Ha, bitch, please. You knew what sort of place this was before coming. Otherwise you wouldn't have come this late at night, huh? Just know your place. Got it?"

She paused now. Some of the more high-brow pronunciations had faded from the man's voice to be replaced by a more street-level form of conversation. The man was playing a role. Just like she was.

Like everyone did in a place like this.

She nodded slowly and then got to her feet. Hoping that the sudden change in posture might provide new perspective. To get the man's guard down even further.

She leaned forward, resting one hand on the desk and studying the fire, then glanced back. "It doesn't scare you?" she said. "That I'm charged with murder?"

"What's your name again?" he said, frowning at her.

She shrugged. "Sparkles. Pixie. Silver. Whatever."

He smirked. "Smartass. Cute ass." He winked.

Again, her skin crawled. She turned to face him now, arms crossed over her less-than-flattering sweater. "It doesn't scare you?" she repeated.

She stressed the word *scare.*

With men like this, fear was something they'd deny. It was a matter of pride. The problem with machismo was that it so often entailed a dishonesty of emotional depth. A dishonesty about *felt* reality.

And now, this man was scowling at her.

She'd offended him with the question. Which had partly been the point.

He snapped, his voice like iron, "You think you're the only one who has taken a life?"

She watched him. "So you've done it as well?"

He shrugged, glancing over his shoulder again, his arms crossed but his posture rigid now where he remained leaning in the door. He didn't look like he wanted to respond to this question. He worried at his lip and muttered under his breath.

She realized she had him hooked but only briefly.

She wasn't one for fishing, but she knew the metaphors well enough. Often, conventional wisdom was to reel a fish in slowly once the hook was set.

But sometimes . . . in rare occasions, if the hook was coming free, slow and steady was the wrong play. Sometimes, a sharp, jerking motion was required.

She was in danger. She knew that much. Isolated, in a strip club run by the mob, surrounded by men who were eyeing her in a *certain* way, she could feel the fear.

But she also was here on a mission. Her stomach was churning. The sure sign that anxiety was trying to set root. But she denied it purchase by refocusing.

Refocusing on the man in the door. And she said, suddenly, "I don't believe you!" and added a sneer to her voice. "I think your uncle killed people. Not you. And you're just taking credit for it!"

The sudden change in her tone, the sudden aggression gave the man pause. He stared at her, frozen in place. And then his eyes narrowed briefly.

He glared at her, opened his mouth, closed it again, and lowered his hands, his arms unfurling. He pointed a finger at her in a threatening way. "You think you know so much, do you?" he snapped.

"You're not denying it. Your uncle *has* killed people, hasn't he? Any of his workers? Young women?"

The moment she said it, Artemis knew she'd crossed a line.

The man looked as if he'd been slapped. He froze in place, staring at her. And she spotted something in his gaze.

But then, he snarled, taking a step into the room, like the stalking motion of a hyena. "You don't know what the hell you're talking about. *We* do uncle's wet work. You oughta learn some respect. Come here!"

He was now marching toward her, a vengeance in his eyes.

Artemis panicked, reached back, snatching desperately for a golden pen. As the man crossed the floor, stomping on the wooden floorboards, five paces away, three. . . She knocked over the pens. Snatched one, holding it tight, prepared to jam it into his eye.

And then, a voice from behind them.

"Excuse me. What's going on?"

Both of them froze. For a moment, Artemis didn't move. Standing still, shivers trembling down her back.

The voice had a faint accent, and was smooth and soft. The sort of voice that conjured images of authority and of a different generation. A suave, charismatic voice.

A voice, in a way, that hinted at her father. Not *quite*. But certainly the same undertones of control and authority.

But unlike her father, *this* voice belonged to a man who had the tools and power to *act* on his authority.

She turned sharply, looking Randy Cortez in the eyes and going suddenly still.

CHAPTER 17

The owner of *Heads and Tails* was watching her. Unlike his nephews, he didn't wear expensive clothing but was dressed simply in a sweater and slacks. His hair was longer, slicked back, and he boasted a well-oiled, curving goatee.

The man looked her directly in the eye and folded his hands in front of him. He had stepped from behind the fireplace. She wondered how many times he'd performed this little stunt in order to impress people in his office. The fireplace had opened like a door, revealing a secret room beyond. The room extended into a hall and moved further down, toward, by the look of things, what appeared like a staircase in the back. She spotted a man lingering at the top of the staircase. The other twin.

But then, without so much as a sound, the fireplace rotated and began to close once more.

Randy Cortez looked at her without blinking. He had a pleasant face. His eyes creased in smile lines.

And currently, he was doing exactly this, his teeth just barely visible past his lips as he smiled with a faintly open mouth.

"So I hear you're looking for a job," he said conversationally.

She took a hesitant step away from the man's nephew, distancing herself, still gripping the pen.

Cortez glanced down, still unblinking, and spotted where the golden pens had strewn across his table. He looked up again. The smile remained.

It was the smile of a car salesman. But an experienced one. The sort of salesman who, after so many years, began to believe in the way in which they manipulated the emotions of others. Eventually even convincing themselves that they were engaging in something authentic.

And again, she was reminded vaguely of her father.

The man she had thought was the Ghost-killer.

And now, facing this new threat, she wondered just how mistaken she had been.

Was *this* the real killer?

She swallowed faintly. She said, "I was wanting to speak to you, Mr. Cortez."

The albino nephew had shuffled back now, sheepish, lingering in the door.

He turned, as if beginning to leave, but Cortez said, "Hang on. Don't go."

There was a finality to those words. Implying in the tone itself that there was no point in questioning them. The man remained in the doorway, frozen suddenly. The rage depleted from his face, and along with it, some of the blood seemed to have left as well. Now, he remained motionless, staring, stuck in place. He let out a small, rattling breath.

Artemis could feel the fear. She could feel her own ebbing and flowing.

Again, she wanted to turn and run.

Now, Cortez was watching her. "I know who you are, Artemis Blythe."

She gritted her teeth. A slow trickle of fear trembled down her spine. So many people seemed to know who she was.

She said, "And you know I have nowhere else to go."

He watched her like a shark watching a minnow. "What was it you two were just talking about before I came in?"

Again, she shared a look with the twin. His gaze didn't linger, though, preferring to look off over his shoulder, as if completely disinterested in the occurrences inside the room.

"Nothing," Artemis said slowly.

The man frowned. "Nothing often means something. What was it?"

Artemis hid a grimace. If she was right, then this man was the one who'd been killing those women twenty years ago. This man very easily could have been the real Ghost-killer. And if not, he may have had a hand in framing her father for the crimes.

She leaned back as he gestured at the red padded chair.

"Have a seat," he murmured softly.

She complied cautiously, lowering herself into the cushioned chair. Her pulse quickened, and blood bruited through her veins.

She was immediately aware of the hush and stillness of the room. The space seemed smaller now, cramped, and the walls, she realized, weren't nearly so ornate, as they were covered in paper-thin wallpaper. The only sound that broke the silence came from the steady hum of a dying fluorescent lightbulb over the man's shoulder, humming above the rotating fireplace.

The man standing behind the desk looked as if he had been expecting her. He was pale and still, and he didn't blink. He watched her intently but said nothing. His eyes were a deep, dark abyss that seemed to swallow up any surrounding light. They were glazed over, almost dead. They seemed to look at everything except her, but she still felt as if he were staring straight into her soul. Her focus drifted to the man's mouth, his lips dry and cracked like the landscape of Mars.

Artemis felt a chill go up her spine as the man continued to stare. She found his gaze unnerving and uncomfortable. She looked away and shuffled her feet, but his eyes remained fixed on her.

Finally, the man broke the silence. "I can see why you're here," he said. His voice was low and raspy, like he had been smoking too much.

Artemis felt her heart sink in her chest. She was suddenly very aware of her presence in the room and of the man's eyes boring into her.

"You don't have to say anything," the man continued. "I know why you're here."

Artemis tried to remain calm, but she could feel her heart racing. She was sure the man could sense her fear.

The man leaned forward in his chair and rested his elbows on the desk. He looked directly at Artemis and smiled. "I know why you're here, and I'm not going to do anything about it."

She hesitated, staring at him, pausing then stuttering, "I—I don't know what you mean."

But he nodded knowingly, tapping a finger against his nose, then pointing that same finger at her. Finally, he blinked—there was an owlish quality to the way he did it.

He leaned back, crossing his arms and studying her closely.

"You want my help, yes?" he said softly.

She blinked.

He tapped a finger to his nose a second time but this time paused to scratch. He smirked. "You are in trouble, Artemis. I've seen on the news. I'm impressed. . ." he added slowly, then chuckled. "You know. . . I'm a bit of a chess player myself."

And suddenly, as if by magic, he'd procured something small and rectangular from behind his desk. There was a scraping sound of a wooden drawer opening and closing.

Then the faintest of clicks as the small chessboard was placed between them and opened slowly. Unhinged and then spread like a book.

Slowly, meticulously, the man placed the pieces in their starting spots.

"I've heard you are one of the best to come from Washington State," he said simply. He nodded. "I've watched some of your games with interest."

She hesitated, unsure if she ought to be alarmed or flattered.

She cleared her throat. "I . . . I see. . ."

He smiled, his eyes wrinkling. He gave her a glance, an almost grandfatherly look. And then, he murmured. "Don't be afraid. . . You're here for a job, is that right?"

She nodded feverishly.

He said, "But not the sort of job you implied to my nephews."

She paused, uncertain. But then shook her head.

He chuckled now, crossing his arms. "Your brother, Tommy . . . he dropped you off?"

She wasn't sure where this was going now, but she felt as if she was treading in dangerous territory. More prickles erupted up and down her spine. "I . . . he's not involved," she said simply.

He looked at her, raising an eyebrow. "You're among friends here, Artemis. Your father and I have had . . . dealings in the past."

And as he said it, he sat slowly, reclining in an equally luxurious and plush chair behind his desk. The fire flickered behind him, casting the warm glow over the red chair, along the table, giving him the look of a man sitting on a throne made of flame.

Cortez said simply, "You need my protection. You need fake identities. Money. A job . . . friends? These things, yes?" He looked at her. He didn't wait for her to answer, as if so certain of his conclusion that there was no point waiting for a response. He looked down again, giving a little snort. "Yes. . . Yes, I know it's true."

Her heart pounded hard against her ribcage. She paused, taking in the luxurious details of the ornate desk by the fireplace. Some small wooden carvings littered the underside of the table. She frowned at these and then bit her lip slowly.

The carvings were of strange, disconcerting glyphs. Unlike any she'd seen before.

The man seated in the luxurious stuffed chair watched her as he finished setting up the chessboard. The chessboard rested between them, black and white pieces set in perfect symmetry.

She tried to rise to her feet now. Hesitating and saying, "You know . . . maybe I should leave." She waved toward the door.

Instead of even entertaining this thought, though, the man gestured to the chair opposite him. "Please," he said. "Take a seat."

There was no room for questioning.

She slowly walked over and sat down, her body tense with anticipation. Would she make it out of this room alive?

The man began to speak, his voice calm and measured. "I will be honest with you. If you win, I will offer you a job. If you lose, you will be dead by morning. Your fate lies in the balance."

She blinked. He didn't.

He spoke so matter-of-factly, as if there was nothing more obvious in the world. As he watched her and smiled, he gave the faintest of shrugs.

She leaned back in the chair. "I. . . Excuse me?"

He shrugged again. "As I said. My move."

She winced, hesitating, glancing over her shoulder. The albino twin in the door was watching her closely. The second twin had returned, having made his way back through the halls, and was now lurking in the hall *behind* his brother.

As she stared out of the room, despite her anxiety, she noticed something else. The room seemed ornate and luxurious, but the hall beyond was far, far less so. Cold, bare, without so much as a carpet or lighting of any kind.

The flames from the fireplace continued to cast odd shadows over the room, through the hall.

Artemis glanced at the chessboard. She slowly placed her hands on her lap. She wasn't concerned about winning. She'd beaten some of the best in her time.

But she couldn't quite see what *he* was playing at.

The man smiled and gestured to the board. "Let us begin."

He reached out and moved one of his pieces. His movements were smooth and confident, as if he had done this thousands of times before.

The woman watched him intently, trying to analyze his strategies.

She focused on the board, trying to predict her opponent's moves. Her hands trembled as she reached for one of her pieces and moved it across the board.

The man nodded in approval. "Very good," he said.

The woman could feel her heart pounding in her chest as she continued the game. Every move seemed to be a risk, and one wrong move could cost her life. But she was determined to play her best.

Back and forth they went, their moves carefully calculated. With each passing turn, the tension in the room was palpable.

Artemis' fingers trembled over her queen. She spotted it easily enough.

The man was good. Perhaps even a 1900, maybe 2000. But she'd been a grandmaster for most of her adult life. Ranked in the 2800s. Her lifetime goal had often been to achieve 3000—the first human to ever accomplish this feat.

But now, as she stared at the table, she wasn't so sure this goal mattered.

She moved another piece, sliding it. As she did, she said simply, "I . . . I need some help, maybe. But. . ."

She trailed off, watching as he castled, moving his king over his rook. He adjusted the pieces and then gestured at her as if to say, *your move.*

She said, "I . . . I know you have connections. Tommy did tell me that."

"Your brother is a man of connections himself."

She winced, remembering all the warnings Tommy had given her about acceptable subjects for conversation. But at this point, she wasn't interested in what Tommy thought.

He'd gone and abandoned her, hadn't he?

Where was he?

She shot a look toward the doorway, but Tommy was still absent. She returned her attention to the man in question.

"I. . ." she paused. Moved a piece. Two moves and she would have him. What was he playing at? Was this some power move?

She looked up, studying him, and realized he was smiling again.

He was having fun.

That was it.

As simple as that.

Fun.

The reason they were playing. . . *Fun*.

Was this how he'd seen it when targeting those young women? Was he the Ghost-killer? Had he framed her father for *fun*?

Mr. Kramer, Jamie's father, had claimed he'd gone and *seen* the Ghost-killer in person. She hadn't known who he'd meant at the time. But maybe Mr. Kramer had found out the truth.

Maybe Kramer had done some digging of his own, much like Helen had.

But Artemis' thoughts drifted from her sister, from Jamie, refocusing on the chessboard. She thought of her favorite analysts, the Washingtons. Cynthia and Henry Washington had been drugged by Fake-Helen back at Jamie's ranch.

But not killed. Not harmed.

Why?

The FBI agent named Butcher had been killed. But the Washingtons had been left unharmed . . . was there a reason for this?

Was she overthinking it.

She moved her queen again, capturing a knight and ending up on the side of a pawn, which would have been an *en passant* position had the queen been a pawn herself and had the pawn just moved. But now, there was nothing to block the queen's attack on the h-file pawn. Nothing to block her bishop's reinforcement.

The game was already over.

He looked up at her, impressed, nodding. "Well then. . ." he said simply. He chuckled, leaned in, and toppled his king. He then reached across the table. "Good game," he said.

She wasn't getting anywhere.

She could feel her irritation now. Fear replaced by frustration. Time was running out.

And so, she took his hand in a tight grip, her fingers near his wrist, gauging his pulse. She met his smile and looked him in the eye.

And then, breathing slowly, deciding that subtlety was the game of a woman who had the luxury of time, she summoned her nerve and blurted out, "Are you the real Ghost-killer?"

She held his wrist. She felt his pulse.

He blinked a single time, staring at her. And then, he frowned, beginning to reply. His pulse didn't change. But his eyes had narrowed in irritation.

His hand felt cold to her touch, despite the fire behind them. She watched his eyes, the pupils, felt his pulse.

No change. No surprise, just irritation.

"What are you nattering about?" he said, pulling his hand back and wiping it against the table.

But she was now standing, staring at him, careful and watchful. She wasn't sure what her escape route was, yet. And it didn't matter.

She needed the truth.

She'd already put herself in danger. Jumping from the frying pan into the fire. But now. . . Now she felt certain that the only way for her to solve this was to take the direct approach.

He'd thought she was here for a job. Fearful of reprisal for the murder of Azin Kartov. . .

She'd hoped by catching him off guard, by surprise, he might reveal something. But he looked more irritated than called out.

She could feel her heart sinking. She said, "I know you framed my father for the murder of those girls."

187

Again, she *knew* no such thing.

But she was fishing.

And again, he didn't react. At least, not at first. But then, those smiling eyes turned into a frowning expression, his dark brow lowering slowly.

"Excuse me?" he said. And then he looked past her at his nephews. "What is this shit?"

Both of the twins were shrugging, shaking their heads and trying to avoid their uncle's gaze. He returned his attention to her. "You come in *here.* . . And try *that*? What the hell are you talking about, Blythe?"

She paused, staring at him.

But he wasn't done. She kept cataloging, watching his reaction. She could feel his anger. Could feel the danger closing in, but she couldn't afford to *think* like that. She had to be patient, to wait.

And now, all semblance of calm and control had faded. His anger was palpable as he snapped, "You're trying to stitch me up!"

"You didn't say no," she said firmly.

"Are you wired?" he said suddenly, gaping. "Shit—did you check her for wires?" he yelled at his nephews.

"You said you didn't want us handling the girls again," said one of the young men, shrugging.

But now the uncle was retreating, hastening away, his back to the bookcase. He was staring at Artemis, wide-eyed, then waving a hand as if to gesture his nephews toward her. "She's wired, dammit!" Now he was yelling. He shouted *at* her, though not *to* her, "I haven't killed anyone! I'm innocent! It's a lie! It's all a lie!"

"I'm not wired!" she said quickly, stumbling back, hands spread out.

But then, the two twins hemmed her into the room.

She retreated around the table, still clutching her golden pen. But Mr. Cortez moved as well, hastening around the other side, chased by her, still shouting, "I never did it! It's a lie! I deny everything!"

She wasn't sure what to think of this. Wasn't sure if she believed him or not.

But now, she'd trapped herself in a wolves' den with a few snarling beasts.

Her back touched against the rotating fireplace.

And then it opened.

One moment, she'd been retreating from the two twins. The next, she began to spin, the ground beneath her rotating like a plate.

"Come on!" Tommy's voice shouted from behind her.

She looked back sharply, stunned to realize her brother was standing in the dark, gray tunnel she'd spotted earlier *behind* the ornate desk.

"Blythe!" screamed Cortez. "You asshole!"

And then came the gunshots. Cortez had ripped a weapon from his hand, aimed—

But Tommy snatched his sister by the wrist and yanked her bodily into the hall behind the fireplace, dragging her forward.

Gunshots rang out. Bits of plaster erupted above her head. But Tommy was now dragging her.

Confusion reigned briefly.

And then the two of them burst down the stairs, fleeing the room.

"Go after them!" screamed Cortez. "Go! Go!"

She heard the sound of pursuing footsteps as the nephews gave chase.

Tommy breathed heavily at her side, tugging her along.

"Where were you!" she snapped, gasping as they took the next flight of stairs in the dark hall.

"Getting evidence," he shot back. "Now shut up and run!"

CHAPTER 18

They knew that their lives were in danger, and they had to do everything they could to escape the clutches of the two gunmen who were hot on their trail.

Unlike the luxurious office space, the building they were in was old and decrepit, with peeling wallpaper and creaky floorboards. Artemis led the way, her heart pounding in her chest as she raced down the narrow hallway, her brother following close behind.

She could hear the gunmen's footsteps echoing behind them, growing louder and more frenzied with each passing moment. They were getting closer, and Artemis knew that they had to think of something fast.

She glanced around frantically, looking for any way out. The windows were too small to crawl through, and the door at the end of the hallway was locked tight.

Suddenly, an idea struck her. She grabbed Tommy by the hand and pulled him toward the door of a nearby supply closet. They tumbled inside, and Artemis frantically searched for a way to barricade the door.

She found a pile of old brooms and mops and began shoving them against the door, hoping to buy them some time. Tommy helped her, his hands shaking with fear as they worked to secure the barricade.

For a moment, they were safe. They crouched in the darkness of the supply closet, listening to the muffled sounds of the gunmen as they stormed through the building, searching for their quarry.

But Artemis knew that it was only a matter of time before they were found. She had to come up with a plan, and fast.

She racked her brain, trying to think of a way out. Dust itched at her nose. Her fingers were layered in the stuff from handling the brooms. The two of them exhaled deeply, breaths coming hurried as they lingered in the darkness.

And then she spotted it.

Above.

Urgently, she pointed it out to Tommy, and together they began to push and pull at the grate of the ventilation shaft. The sort of shaft found in old, run-down buildings just like this one. The two of them continued to pry, trying to loosen it from its moorings. It was stuck fast, but they kept at it, desperation fueling their efforts.

Finally, with a loud *creak*, the grate came loose. Artemis boosted Tommy up into the shaft and then followed him, pulling the grate back into place behind her.

They crawled through the shaft, their progress slow and awkward as they made their way through the twists and turns. Artemis' heart was in her throat the entire time, half expecting the gunmen to burst into the closet at any moment and discover their escape route.

She heard footsteps. Thumping.

Then . . . gunshots.

The loud tinny sound of metal being struck by metal.

She cursed, dragging at Tommy's arm. "They're below us—shooting!"

"Quiet," he whispered back.

The two of them slipped along the shaft, moving hurriedly. Tommy had to pause, reaching out with a clothed elbow to slam into a rotating fan in the center, blocking their progress.

The darkness was soon all encompassing. Artemis couldn't see more than a couple of inches, and these provided only by the light glowing from Tommy's phone.

"Where are we going?" she whispered.

"Out," he whispered back.

His phone flashed, and she heard more shouting.

"Where were you?" she repeated.

But again, he ignored her.

The two of them crawled onward, moving through the dark. And then, Artemis spotted light.

She pointed, urgently. An opening.

One by one, they shimmied through. Tommy first, then Artemis.

They dropped onto a cheap plastic table below, which was soldered to the ground. And Artemis realized they were in the main attraction of *Heads and Tails*.

They dismounted from the table, avoiding the stage and the poles spread throughout the room. Everything was now silent. Tommy and Artemis crept through the shadows of the abandoned strip club, the darkness deepening around them. They each pointed simultaneously toward the glowing red *Exit* sign above a door. The air was thick with stale smoke, and more than one surface glittered with what looked like a dusting of fool's gold.

The club was silent now, its lights long gone out, the dance floor and colorful stage decorations replaced by a morbid, sad emptiness.

They were both as quiet as they could be, their movements cautious and deliberate, every step taken with care.

Artemis spotted movement behind them.

The twins were visible through a window, just *outside* the strip club, patrolling the perimeter, their flashlights shining through the glass and making the darkness inside seem even more oppressive. Tommy and Artemis held their breath, both afraid that the slightest sound could give them away.

Tommy nudged her, moving away from the exit toward a staircase on the opposite side of the room. "Balcony exit," he whispered. "I know the way."

"You know this place?" she whispered back, trying to keep her tone free of accusation.

"Sue me," he muttered. "Come on—balcony's this way. They won't see us."

She followed. They made their way around the perimeter of the club, avoiding the lights and knowing that the guards might well, at any moment, spot them in the shadows. As they moved, their eyes adjusted to the night, and they began to make out the details of the club's interior.

The walls were lined with faded velvet curtains, and the floor was covered in a thick carpet that had once been bright and luxurious. A grand piano sat in the corner of the room, its keys still gleaming in the dark.

The dance floor was lined with booths, the tables still in place, but the chairs had been moved to the side, creating a clear path for the clientele.

At the far end of the room, they reached the staircase leading up to a second level. There was a curtain across the entrance to the stairs, blocking their view of whatever lay beyond.

Tommy and Artemis moved cautiously as they made their way up the stairs. They stopped at the top, peering through the curtain and into the darkness beyond.

The second level was lined by a long hallway, with a number of small doorways leading into what appeared to be private rooms. The walls were draped with thick red velvet, and the air was still and heavy with the smell of smoke.

Tommy and Artemis crept through the hallway, the darkness growing thicker with each step. They paused at the doors of the private rooms, not wanting to risk being seen.

Eventually, they reached the end of the hall, where a door opened up to a small balcony overlooking the club. Artemis peered through the glass, her eyes widening as she took in the sight below.

The lights from the guards' patrols shone brightly in the night sky, and the club seemed like a ghost town. But the guards were still scanning the streets, the parking lot.

Tommy and Artemis looked at each other, their faces illuminated by the moonlight. A gentle breeze blew through their hair, and they shared a moment of understanding before stepping out onto the balcony.

Neither of them spoke.

Now came the tricky part. They'd be exposed for a brief moment before dropping over the balcony.

The air was cold on her skin as she pushed through the balcony door. Then, Tommy and Artemis moved *fast*.

Both darting forward.

A shout. A gunshot.

Glass exploded behind them.

No point in silence, now. Artemis yelled.

And together, with Tommy, she jumped from the balcony, aiming toward the ground twelve feet below.

"Tuck!" Tommy had time to yell.

But Artemis was just trying to avoid face-planting. She hit the ground and rolled. Tommy followed. Pain lanced up her foot, her ankle. She hissed in pain.

But she pushed to her feet, gingerly testing her weight.

Tommy dragged at her, pulling her forward, and together the two of them hastened away from the space under the balcony, moving rapidly off into the woods.

Tommy tugged at her arm, and Artemis followed quickly. She winced a few times, running on her leg, but the shouts from behind them faded as they disappeared into the woods behind the strip club, hastening into the shadows of the surrounding mountains.

"I found something," Tommy said as they ran, breathing desperately.

Sweat prickled her forehead, and she glanced at him, frowning.

"You're going to want to see it."

CHAPTER 19

Jamie Kramer shivered in the dark. His wrists ached, the ropes binding them biting off the circulation. He glanced toward where his sister was curled up beneath a small blanket. She was trembling, quiet, trying to sleep.

But Sophie hadn't slept in a few days.

He could see the way her eyes fluttered, and she opened them to stare into every dark corner at the sound of movement.

He could feel the motion. The cold metal of the storage compartment at his back. Sliding occasionally whenever the truck moved.

He wasn't sure what sort of vehicle they were in. He'd been unconscious when he was brought here. And they had been on the move ever since.

Now, he listened to the engine grumble beneath him. He could feel the tires wearing over the asphalt.

His heart pounded, and his breath came in short gasps. Fear had been his constant companion over the last few days.

From where Jamie sat in the back of the semi-truck, his hands bound tightly behind his back, he couldn't help but feel a creeping sense of dread. The darkness inside the truck was absolute, and he couldn't see much more than Sophie's shape. He strained to hear any sound that might give him a clue about what was happening, but the only noise was the faint hum of the truck's engine.

Suddenly, he heard a voice. It was low and raspy, and it seemed to be coming from somewhere in front of him. "Who are you?" he shouted, hoping to get some kind of response.

He couldn't see anything.

But the voice came slowly, creepily. "I am your captor," the voice replied, its tone dripping with malice. "And you are my prisoner. You will do exactly as I say or suffer the consequences."

The man's pulse quickened with fear.

He swallowed faintly. "Wh-what do you want?"

He shifted again, and his head bumped against something dangling above him. He turned and after a second realized he was staring at a radio dangling from a wire.

The voice was coming from here.

"Tell me what you know about Artemis Blythe," the voice said softly.

Jamie struggled against the ropes that bound him, failing to reply. The name of Artemis sent a jolt of longing through his chest.

He could feel his heart pounding, could feel his breath coming quickly.

He had been sitting in the back of the truck for what felt like days, trying to wriggle free from the knots that held him tightly in place. His wrists and ankles ached from the strain of his efforts, but he refused to give up. He had to get out of there. He had to help Sophie.

A faint hum filled the air as the engine of the truck hit a higher gear, and Jamie felt a jolt as the vehicle began to pick up speed.

"I asked you a simple question," the voice said over the speaker.

Again, he didn't reply. Their captor wasn't exactly the sort one *spoke* with.

Now, he tried to get his bearings, but it was impossible to tell where they were headed. The truck had no windows, and he had no way of knowing where the sun was in the sky.

As the truck rumbled on, Jamie's thoughts turned to Artemis. He had no idea why this captor wanted to know about her, but he knew he couldn't give them what they wanted. Artemis was a close friend, and he would do anything to protect her. She was . . . more than a friend.

Much more.

In a way, Artemis was his childhood.

In a way, Artemis was someone he wished he could be like. He'd never known anyone as smart as her. Or as brave.

His skin felt cold, and he let out a deep breath.

He wasn't very brave. He'd never felt brave at all.

He could hear Sophie's breath coming in quick, panicked gasps. He whispered, "It's going to be okay, Soph. It's going to be alright."

She pretended like she hadn't heard, like she was still asleep.

The sound of a speaker crackling to life again startled Jamie out of his thoughts. A singsong, playful voice filled the air, echoing off the metal walls of the truck.

"I know you know about Artemis, Jamie. You have two choices. You can tell me about your time with her, or you can suffer the consequences. And believe me, the consequences will not be pleasant."

Jamie's heart raced as he weighed his options. He knew he couldn't give them what they wanted, but he also knew he couldn't withstand much more of this. The ropes were cutting into his skin, and his head pounded from the lack of food and water.

He took a deep breath and tried to steady his voice. "I don't know where Artemis is," he said firmly. "I haven't seen her in days. You *know* this!"

The speaker crackled again, and the voice let out a low, sinister laugh. "I'm not sure you understand the situation, Jamie. Tell me what you know. What does she like—is she the same as she was when she was ten? Have you two made love?"

Jamie felt his cheeks warm.

Another little giggle. "I'm sorry—was that *too personal*?" the voice whispered. "You should tell me what I want to know, Jamie... No? Hmm... We'll see how long you can hold out. We have plenty of time to break you."

The truck came to a stop, and Jamie's heart sank as he heard the sound of the front door opening. He knew what was coming next.

His heart pounded. He stared toward the back of the truck, panic in his heart. "Sophie... Sophie, just stay quiet, okay. Whatever happens. Stay quiet!"

He heard footsteps, whistling.

And then...

Nothing.

He frowned, staring at the back of the truck, expecting the doors to open at any moment.

But they remained sealed shut.

A few moments passed, and then—the truck still quiet, motion-less—the voice returned. Still over the speaker.

"You can make this easy on yourself, Jamie," it hissed. "Just tell us about Artemis, and we'll let you go. It's that simple."

We. Not *me.* *We.* This woman was working for someone. He felt a tremble along his arms and let out a leaking breath.

Jamie closed his eyes and prayed for a miracle. He couldn't hold out much longer, but he knew he couldn't give in. Artemis was counting on him. He just hoped it wouldn't be too late.

He shifted again, his back against the cold metal, the speaker crackling above him.

But he didn't speak.

He didn't know *what* this psycho wanted with Artemis, but he knew he couldn't give in. And so, he waited, quiet, motionless, trembling and very afraid.

Where was Artemis?

A faint flicker of hope. Was she okay? Did she miss him?

He shook his head, dropping his gaze and staring at the metal floor beneath him. And then the sound of a slamming door.

The truck rumbled back to life.

And they were on the move once more.

CHAPTER 20

Artemis and Tommy had come to a stop by an old rusted oil tanker, which had been left in the forest. Around the tanker, Artemis spotted other discarded pieces of debris. It looked like a junkyard; that had been cleared out and the remaining residue overgrown.

Artemis glanced toward her brother, watching him carefully and waiting as he pulled out a small flash drive from his pocket and held it up for her to see.

The two of them stood in the woods, near the old abandoned junkyard. Artemis readjusted her footing as she felt something hard under one shoe and shifted her posture to avoid it. Glancing down, she spotted a large metal screw. She kicked it off to the side and then said, "So what's that?"

"Video feed and employee logs," Tommy replied simply.

She stared at her brother.

Now that he wasn't wearing those stupid sunglasses, she realized the reason he'd been hiding his eyes. The mismatched colors of blue and gold were marred in addition by a small circle of black that had bruised his left eye.

He reached up, gingerly massaging this eye while simultaneously extending the small flash drive to her. "Hold this," he said.

She did, cautiously, watching as he removed a small cable from his pocket. After a few seconds, he'd attached the cable adapter to his phone, then clicked his fingers, accepting the flash drive back, inserting it into the adapter, and turning so she could now see his screen.

"Sorry it took me so long back there," he muttered, jerking his head vaguely over his shoulder.

She was still frowning at him. Already, tonight, she'd been chased by a homicidal cop and hunted by armed albinos. She wasn't in a very placid mood. But now, as she stared at the glowing screen which reflected off the red-dappled tanker, she said carefully, "What is this?"

"Yeah. . ." he scratched at his chin. And left the word there, though it wasn't an answer to her question.

So she tried again while he fumbled with the buttons on his screen. "Tommy, you left me back there to die."

"What? Hell no. They wouldn't have killed you."

"They sure seemed like it."

206

But Tommy shook his head. "Nah. They knew who you were. Woulda used you to get at me. But this way. . ." he chuckled. "Reverse uno."

"What?" She paused, frowned, realizing she was asking this question a bit too much. So instead, cautiously, she said, "You slunk off to steal *this*? Using me as bait?"

He shot her a look, shrugged. "We needed evidence, yeah? Solid proof."

She sighed slowly. Part of her wanted to slap him. And then all of her wanted to. So she did. Not on the face, but she did plant a solid one on his shoulder, registering her disapproval.

He snorted, rubbed at his arm, but then clicked a file, pulling up something. "Be pissed if you want, but I found something."

She leaned in, deciding that the slap had alleviated *some* of her irritation with her unpredictable brother.

He was saying, "I knew where Cortez kept the security room. Late at night, the twins are the only patrol. So I figured getting them out early would give me a back entry in."

"So you *did* use me as bait."

"Whatever, look here." He was tapping a half-gloved finger against the screen, indicating a file he'd pulled up. "See that? Internal memo."

She leaned in, studying the information, hesitating only briefly. "What . . . is it?"

"Insurance claim for an employee."

"So?"

"Look closer," he said, gruff now. He paused. "Should mention, Cortez isn't the Ghost-killer."

"Wait, how do you know?"

"Because he's on camera when she died."

"When who died?"

"Just *look* will you. It's not Cortez. The security footage shows him in his office the date she died."

"The date who. . ."

"Just *look*!" her brother repeated again, irritated.

She did. And then she blinked. There was a picture of the employee in question. A young woman with bronze curls. A pretty face. A woman who didn't *quite* look like Helen Blythe but shared *some* similar features. Enough similarities that it caught Artemis' attention.

"Hang on. . ." she said. "What sort of insurance claim?"

"Girl died," said Tommy bluntly. He raised the phone a bit, leaning in, the light glowing off his features. "Killed."

"W-when?"

This was when he lowered the phone and looked at her, solemnity in his gaze. "Last year," he said simply.

She froze in place, staring back at him, but then her eyes darting to the screen again, voraciously consuming the text. She scanned the file, settled on the date in question, and gaped at it. "R-really?" she muttered. It was dated nearly eight months ago. "She was killed last year?" Artemis murmured. "But that means. . ."

"Looks a lot like Helen, yeah?"

"That means. . ." Artemis repeated.

Tommy finished her sentence. "Ghost-killer is still active? Maybe has *always* been active but just changed his targets. Prostitutes, strippers—people pay way less attention to them. Young women from affluent neighborhoods? That gets noticed. But people like this. . ." he tapped his finger and winced, and for a moment his eyes flashed in irritation. "No one really cares for our kind."

Artemis was pacing now, shaking her head. She waved a finger as if to say *get on with it*, but really she was mostly speaking to her own mind. She said, "What's the girl's name?"

"Liza," he replied. "Liza O'Dell."

"Is there anything else we know about her?"

"Er . . . legal or illegal?"

"What—like *her* actions?"

"No—do you mind if I get the information . . . you know. The fun way?"

Artemis glanced at her brother, still pacing. "Tommy, we just broke into a strip club. I broke into a police station earlier tonight to grab evidence."

"What'd you find?" he muttered distractedly, doing something on his phone.

"Nothing much. Couple of stupid files and a cord used for the murders."

Tommy looked up sharply. "What type of cord?"

"I . . . does it matter?"

"Rope?"

"N-no. It was like the cord from a computer. An electrical cord."

He turned the phone to her again, the light swishing like the rotating glow of a lighthouse. But then, when she leaned in, Tommy's own impatience took over, and he read the article again and summarized. "Liza O'Dell was strangled by a computer cable," he said simply. "Like I said, when she was murdered, Cortez was on the security footage I checked. It's not him, Artemis. Cortez isn't our guy."

"If not him, then who? But wait, hang on—computer cable?" Artemis went still, staring at him.

The two of them were now both agitated. Both breathing heavily.

"Shit," Artemis said.

"Double shit."

"So dad isn't. . ."

"Isn't the Ghost-killer," Tommy replied, staring. "Because the Ghost-killer is still *out there*."

"And . . . and it can't be Cortez?"

"No—look at the coroner's dating of Liza's death. And see this?" he showed her a security feed of Randy Cortez sitting in his office, feet on the ornate table, swirling a golden pen while chatting on the phone. Her brother tapped the time stamp.

It put him in the same timeframe the coroner provided for the woman's death. "Not him," Tommy said simply. "And not *Dad*."

She shook her head. "But . . . how's. . ." She trailed off, wincing and pacing in agitation in front of the rusted tanker.

She was shaking her head fervently now. Her fingers tapped against the inside of her palm in a drumming pattern. "So if the Ghost-killer is still out there. . . What if there were others?" she said suddenly. "What if the Ghost-killer continued his spree after dad was arrested but just changed the type of victim. Instead of affluent women from the suburbs, what if he started targeting people he thought would be overlooked? Or people in different municipalities. What if he's been active all this time!"

Tommy blinked and then returned to his phone, his fingers a flurry. "I got Dawkins' key to their database, hang on," he said.

Artemis shot a quick look over her shoulder at the name of Dawkins, out of sheer instinct. If ever there was a doom of Damocles in her life, it was that family.

The trembles along her spine only intensified as she thought of the *other* imminent danger that awaited her. It would take time to reach their rendezvous. Two hours . . . tops. Two hours before she needed to meet Fake-Helen and trade for Jamie.

As she thought of Jamie Kramer, her heart fluttered again. Her sympathy was with Sophie and her older brother. She wondered how horrible it must have been for the two of them, trapped in that evil woman's clutches.

She'd thought she'd had it all figured out.

Had thought her own father had hired this psycho to spring him from prison. But what if . . . what if it was someone else. What if the *real* Ghost-killer was the one behind it?

So who was it?

And how could Artemis go into this meeting with Fake-Helen without being sorely outmaneuvered? She couldn't hand her father over now. She couldn't let Fake-Helen escape. But the more information Artemis had, the more *truth* she accrued, the better chance there was of success.

She continued to pace, stomping a foot every few seconds and turning on her heel. It felt like a dance. It felt like the pacing of some hound on the cusp of the hunt.

"So. . ." she said slowly, "Check for other murders. Same criteria. Same age. White women, brown or bronze hair. Strangled by an electrical cord. Can you do that?"

"Umm . . . yeah, keyword stuff. One sec." Her brother continued to type, and she continued to stave off the rising sense of doom.

Her heart continued to throb in her chest. She muttered to herself as she paced and then looked over as her brother gave a shaky inhale.

"What is it?"

"Three others," he said.

"Only three?"

"Yeah. Only one of them was in Washington. The other was in Salinas, California."

She wrinkled her nose, staring. "And the third?"

"Also in California. A therapist of some kind. But the other two were prostitutes."

"So . . . the Ghost-killer targeted a therapist and two prostitutes. What do they look like?" She approached hurriedly, peering over her brother's shoulder as he continued to click through the case files. After each one, Artemis felt her anxiety ratchet up.

Each face, staring back at her from the dimly glowing screen, was similar to Helen. Each one pretty, each one with bronze hair, curled. Each of them with intelligent eyes, despite where they'd ended up.

Artemis was shaking her head now, trembling where she stood. "Shit," she whispered. "So . . . the Ghost-killer has still been active. That's his work! It has to be. Strangled with an electrical cord, and all of them look like Helen!"

"Yeah . . . yeah, see this one, Liza, was last year. This one was four years ago, the therapist. And before that. . . This other prostitute, a woman named Starlet. That was eight years ago."

Artemis stood in place, arms crossed in a defensive posture. She could feel the fear rising in her chest. Could feel her breath coming in scattered puffs. She wanted to turn and hide.

She didn't know *what* she wanted.

"Dammit, Tommy. So the Ghost-killer is out there. What if. . . what if Dad hired someone to make it look like—"

"Nah. You don't believe that."

"He had influence, Tommy!" she yelled, facing her brother, arms still crossed. He glared at her. Their mismatched eyes, now facing each other, matched. The blue to blue, the gold to gold. Both of them were shifting foot to foot. Tommy had lowered his phone and was waving it like a nun's disapproving finger under his nose at her.

"Dad didn't do this."

"What if he did?"

"He didn't. You know he didn't. Why wouldn't he have *ever* brought it up? Ever had it pointed out. If he'd been trying to create an alibi for himself, he would've told the DA. The warden. Someone!"

"Maybe. . . Maybe he. . ." She bit her lip but then quailed. Tommy was right. If their father had been hiring someone to act like a copycat, he would've instantly tried to clear his name. There was no reason for him to stay behind bars. He'd hated the experience.

And now . . . now he was free.

Why go to the trouble of hiring Fake-Helen? No. . . No, Artemis realized. It was all too much. She was missing some big piece of the puzzle. And she was beginning to fear that she knew *where* to find it, only she didn't want to.

And suddenly, as she stalked back and forth, shivering, something registered.

She said, "Hang on . . . those three victims. . ." She trailed off, shaking her head.

"What is it?" Tommy said, watching her shrewdly. "What's wrong?"

"N-nothing. . ." she murmured. "Just. . ." She paused, exhaled shakily, then said, "Actually. . ." She closed her eyes, trying to think. "Why so sporadically, then?"

"Self-control?" Tommy shot back.

"What?"

"Maybe the Ghost-killer has been trying to control himself but failing. So the kills are *less* frequent but still there. He's trying to stop but can't."

Artemis huffed. "I . . . I don't. . . Something doesn't add up."

"What is it?"

She closed her eyes, desperately trying to piece it all together. Trying to *think*. But nothing made sense. Not without the missing piece. And now, standing there, bone-tired and exhausted, she felt as if she knew *where* she might be able to find the final clue.

But she'd never been able to discern the truth from him.

Still . . . she had to.

"I need to speak with Dad," she murmured, in the tone of someone suggesting a trip to the gallows. "Right now."

"Why?"

"Because," she shot back, "I. . . Oh God. . . I hope I'm wrong."

"What?"

"I think. . . I think I know who the Ghost-killer is."

Tommy stared at her, frozen in place only briefly. But then he began to move, raising the phone, placing a call.

And Artemis followed her brother's thin, sinewy form as he moved once more through the trees, gesturing for her to fall into step.

CHAPTER 21

Artemis stood facing the small concrete structure where her father was being kept. Behind her, she spotted where her brother lingered back, speaking with the two men he'd left to guard the place. She returned her attention to the enclosure, her breath coming in slow spurts.

Her fingers tingled where she left them at her side, and she shifted faintly, her feet scraping through the pine needles at her feet.

Her one hand extended, lingering on the cold door handle to the shed.

Her brother had already unlocked the door. Now, she'd returned to the old construction zone where her brother and his accomplices had made camp. At night, things seemed different.

The darkness stretched across the horizon, bathing the sky in ink and blotting out even the glimpse of cloud cover. Everything was cast in shadow, including Artemis' heart.

She could feel it straining in her chest, like the weak wings of a fluttering bird attempting to take flight once more but failing liftoff.

She'd been frozen in place, gripping the handle for what felt like a full minute. Now, her back prickled, and she felt the attention of her brother and his goons from where they lingered near an old corrugated metal fence that encircled this holding cell.

She finally mustered up her nerve.

Her father had the final clue.

The dread in her chest had expanded, and she had a glimpse, the faintest *glimmer* of the truth.

She knew what her father was. Suspected now that he had been framed for the murders. But not by Randy Cortez—she'd seen the footage. Cortez had been on camera during Liza's murder.

Not her father.

Not Cortez.

Someone else.

And she had a sinking suspicion she knew who. But her father had to confirm it.

She opened the door, swinging it wide, and then she stepped in, facing where her father had been left cuffed to the wall through a metal supply shelf.

Except he wasn't there.

She blinked, certain she'd made a mistake. But then her eyes spotted the loose handcuffs draped over the metal shelf, left limp and lying there.

Her eyes darted to the window, which had been pried loose—the glass shattered. She spotted a few shards of glass on the ground and a small spatter of blood, crimson droplets, flecking the window.

She gaped, and then she took a hesitant step into the dark.

"D-Dad?" she tried.

But no response. He was gone. She cursed, hastening forward, stepping onto the rusted box that had been used to give her father access to the window. She poked her head up and over.

And she spotted him.

Movement. Her father running, off in the distance, past a rusted, metal mesh fence. Hastening deeper into the industrial zone, fleeing his children.

"Shit!" she cursed. And she spun on her heel, turning fast and shouting, "He's running! Tommy! He's running!"

She gestured wildly as chaos reigned for a moment. Tommy shouted after her.

"Where?"

"South," she screamed back, pointing.

"That's West, dipshit!" he returned.

"Shut up and grab him!" she yelled, already breaking into a run. She could hear her brother barking instructions to his goons behind her. But she didn't stop to watch. She needed to catch Otto Blythe. He was the only bargaining chip they had. If he escaped now, Jamie and Sophie were as good as dead.

Not only that . . . but Artemis wouldn't be able to solve this thing.

She needed the final clue—needed to confront her father and get him to tell the truth for one damn time in his life!

An impossible ask, perhaps.

But in order to try, she needed to look him in the eye rather than watch his rubber soles kick up dust as he fled his temporary holding cell.

She cursed, sweat prickling as her arms and legs pumped and she continued in hot pursuit, racing after her father. She reached the metal mesh fence, flinging herself at it and scrambling desperately up, dropping over the other side, her fingers aching. She dropped to the ground, stumbled a couple of steps, and then broke into a sprint, racing toward where she spotted her father fleeing to a tall, gray industrial building. A giant warehouse, by the look of things. Old, dilapidated, and run-down.

"Dad!" she screamed. "Otto—you asshole! Come back here!"

But her father didn't even glance back. He was quite spry for a man his age, and he continued his flight, kicking up dust on the old, worn roads. A few chunks of asphalt were sent skittering a couple hundred paces ahead, where he'd outdistanced her.

She lowered her head, trying not to swallow dust as she panted, sprinting in hot pursuit.

Artemis sprinted through the industrial zone, her heart pounding in her chest as she chased after her estranged father.

The darkened skies watched her as she ran, sweat pouring down her face. She could see Otto up ahead, his lithe, trim frame darting through the maze of crumbling buildings and rusted machinery. He was always fast, but Artemis was determined to catch him. She pushed herself to run faster, her feet pounding the pavement as she chased after him.

As she ran, she could see the old factories and warehouses that had been abandoned long ago. The once bustling area now lay in ruins, the only signs of life coming from the occasional stray dog or rat scurrying through the debris. Artemis felt a sense of despair as she ran through the desolate landscape, but she pushed it aside and focused on her goal.

Otto had always been a master at slipping away, but Artemis was determined to catch him this time. She had spent years hating him. She had grown up with a hole in her heart, always longing for the father who had destroyed everything.

But now? Now everything had changed.

He'd been a liar. Not a killer. He'd been a manipulator, but . . . but he'd also been there for his kids. Provided for them. He'd taken care of them as a single father for years.

And now. . .

She yelled, "Dad! Stop!" He continued hastening forward.

As she ran, she could see Otto up ahead, darting through a junkyard. He was making his way through the piles of twisted metal and discarded machinery, trying to lose her in the maze of debris. But Artemis was not to be deterred. She pushed herself harder, running faster and faster as she chased after him.

The junkyard portion of this industrial zone, in what looked like a town square in ruins, was a chaotic mess, with piles of old cars and machinery towering above her. Artemis had to dodge and weave her way through the debris, her heart racing as she tried to keep up with her father. He was always one step ahead, but she refused to let him slip away again.

Finally, she saw him clambering up a pile of twisted metal. She could see the fear and desperation in his eyes as he looked back at her, but she refused to let him go. She reached out and grabbed hold of his ankle, pulling him back down to the ground.

They tumbled down the pile of metal, landing in a heap on the ground. Pain flared through her arm. She felt as if she'd skinned her knee.

Her father was gasping now, tired and worn.

He slipped on old springs, kicked free, and scrambled forward, desperately disentangling from the mess and moving toward the large gray structure ahead.

He reached the building a few steps ahead of Artemis, but she continued her pursuit.

"Dad!" she said, her voice hoarse. "Stop! Just stop!"

Her father whirled around, his back pressed to a locked metal door. He held out a hand as if to hold his daughter back, but at the same time, she spotted the way his other hand finagled with the metal at his back, trying to pry the padlock free and give access to the building he'd wanted to use as a bolt-hole.

Artemis approached her father slowly, her hand extended as if she were wrangling some beast.

Her father was watching her, his eyes wide, the icy blue of his pupils standing out, suggesting the fear written across the furrows of his brow.

It only took a second, though, for her father to disguise his emotion. He had never been a very vulnerable man. There were few who could lie as well as he could.

Most lies, in her experience, occurred with the use of words.

Her father lied with his body language.

Having decided that he couldn't break through the padlock, he lowered his hand from where it had been fiddling behind his back. There was the sound of clattering metal as the padlock fell back against the door, leaving white scrape marks.

Her father reached out with his hands, adjusting his jumper as if it were an expensive suit.

He sniffed and set his shoulders, taking a sort of nonchalant stance. He ran his fingers through his hair.

He looked at Artemis, and then, in an even, casual tone, as if he hadn't just been running for his life, he said, "Artemis, how are you?"

She didn't reply. She wasn't sure what she would even say if she did. This man, this strange, manipulative man, wasn't the person she had thought he was.

The misrepresentation of her father had sunk its roots deep in her mind.

She hadn't seen him as a provider who was kind to his children. She had seen him as a coldhearted sociopath. A murderer.

And now, she wasn't sure what to say.

The two of them were breathing heavily. Somehow, her father's forehead wasn't slick with sweat, as if he had managed even to avoid perspiring like a normal man.

Artemis, though, could feel the faint sweat on her brow, could feel it trickling slowly down the side of her face.

As she stared at her father, she said, stammering, "I need to ask you something."

Her father finished adjusting and smoothing his jumper. For a moment, she thought he might try to bolt again.

"I'll just keep chasing you," she said. "Right now, you and I are both wanted. It will only be a matter of time before they come for us."

He frowned at her. "My dear daughter," he said slowly. "I've come to realize, over many years, that my fate has already been decided. But if I leave this place before they apprehend me again, perhaps I can take my fate into my own hands. I won't live under the judgment of lesser men." He sniffed, a sneer creeping into his voice.

She sighed. This was the man she knew. Arrogant. Manipulative. Condescending. He had been a thief and a liar his whole life. And yet, she tried to see more. She tried to see the man who had kept the family together. Who had kept his children. Had provided for them. Who had given his daughters chess lessons. Who had trained them in the art of reading people. In the art of manipulation. He had thought, in his own way, that he had been doing them a favor.

Now, as she exhaled briefly, she said, "You really didn't do it?"

He watched her, flashed a quiet look her way. But then he said, "That's what I've been telling you."

And this time, she phrased it without the inflection of the question. "You really didn't do it."

Her father shook his head. But now it was his turn to stare at her with a speculative expression. His eyes narrowed shrewdly. "Correct me if I'm wrong. . ." he said slowly. "I'm almost beginning to get the sense that you might even believe me."

She didn't deny it. She didn't really know what to say.

"I want to believe you. You wouldn't have been that stupid. The camera never faced your bed. Why would it have that night? I thought you hired this woman to spring you from prison. But then you were scared. *Why* were you scared?"

He shrugged.

"Why did everyone in prison think you were the Ghost-killer? Why did Mr. Kramer come and visit you?"

He sniffed again. He adjusted his sleeves. In a way, it was a gesture that she also often did. He said, "It's a dangerous place in there. A reputation had its uses."

She gaped. "You're serious?"

"As a strip search."

She said, "You pretended to be the Ghost-killer in prison for the reputation?"

He shook his head. "I didn't pretend anything. I allowed people to make their own assumptions. Which everyone did. Yourself included, Artemis."

He was lecturing her. She could tell it in the posture, the stern tone of his voice. Just like he used to. He often liked to take the role of teacher. She knew people like this. Who felt it was their job to educate the "stupid" public on all the oh-so-very-*smart* things that they had ever discovered. They saw themselves as wise, clever, and educated. They saw themselves as sophisticated, and they saw the world at large as stupid, clumsy, foolish, and often *evil*; they saw themselves as teachers and everyone else as pupils.

She bit her tongue, feeling a flash of pain; she didn't reply right away.

Instead, after a moment, gathering herself, she said, "Maybe you're right. I did make assumptions. And I'm sorry."

"Sorry?"

She shook her head. "I know it's not much. Trust me. I know it's not. But yes. I'm sorry." The words came slowly, as if it took more than a small amount of resolve to utter them.

Her father crossed his arms.

He let out a long, leaking breath. He said cautiously, "And what are you sorry about?"

She paused. Then she said, "I don't know how I could've ever believed it was you, Dad—but you didn't deserve to be in there for all those years. I'm sorry I didn't believe you. I am."

Her father was still watching her. His eyes still cold. His gaze unwavering.

He gave a little sniff. And then he said, simply, "I accept. But on one condition."

"I don't expect you to accept. It was an injustice. I see that now. Unless you're still lying. Unless you're still making this all up. But there were other victims. After you were in prison. Victims you didn't know about. Or if you did, you never mentioned. You stayed in there for nearly two decades. I can't imagine you did that as a long con. Not even you. There's one thing I know about you; it's that your primary goal is self-preservation."

She could feel the bitterness creeping into her voice now. Why couldn't he have just been an honest man? She would've believed him then, wouldn't she?

She wasn't so sure. It was to her shame, she felt, that it had taken being framed for murder herself to start wondering if the same had happened to him.

The camera over his bed had been moved. Other victims were found outside the prison.

The Ghost-killer was still out there.

"How did that body end up in the bed with you?"

"Someone placed it there," he said simply. As if the answer was so obvious. In a way, the answer *was* obvious. But the conclusion, the specifics, weren't nearly as apparent.

"I can't give you those years back. And even if I *had* believed you, I'm not sure what I could've done, but now there's a chance I might be able to help."

Her father said, "And how's that?"

She shrugged once. "I think I know who the real Ghost-killer is."

"Who?"

She said, "My first thought was the warden. A man named Doler. He framed someone else, once upon a time, for murder. He killed his own daughter, the way that I thought you had done."

Her father made a face like he had been sucking lemons. "I never would've killed Helen. I loved Helen. Even when things got difficult."

She stared at him. "But the more I thought about it, I realized it wasn't Doler. He had access. Had proven he could murder people with impunity. But no, I think it's someone else."

"Who?" Her father was shaking his head.

Artemis said, "Someone that Mr. Kramer would have known to go and visit. Someone the Professor would have wanted to tutor. To train."

"The Professor?"

It felt like an act. But this was because she had already assumed so much. The Professor had been another prolific killer. In her current line of work, aiding the FBI, Artemis encountered far more of these sorts of people than she wanted to.

But the Professor had ties to the Ghost-killer.

Mr. Kramer had ties to the Ghost-killer.

The victims in Pinelake, the Sheriff's first wife—it all was starting to come into place.

But what had clued her in, what made the most sense, were the names of the victims that had been found after her father had been incarcerated.

No, she realized. That wasn't *exactly* true. It wasn't their names. It was something else entirely.

But she still wasn't sure. And so, she said, "Do you know who did it?"

Her father stared at her.

He didn't reply. He just frowned briefly.

This was the question she had been waiting to ask. This was the question she couldn't have done over the phone.

And this was the question it had all been leading up to.

Did Otto Blythe know who the Ghost-killer was?

He had many contacts in prison. There were many opportunities for others to tell him. But that wasn't the reason she was asking.

Her father was a liar.

But she had to read him now. She had to find the truth.

After a moment, after shaking his head, letting his silver curls fall back in place, her father said, his voice sincere, his eyes full of fear, "No. I don't. That's the problem."

She stared at her father, and her heart sunk.

She could feel her skin prickling. Could feel the fear settling in. Falling like a weight. "Holy shit," she said, unable to avoid the sibilant hiss. She shook her head. She repeated the oath.

Her father stared at her. "What? Who is it?"

She pointed at his face.

"Me?"

But she shook her head. And then the guilt came. She had completely misjudged him. Completely. "I'm so sorry," she said, stammering.

"Artemis, I apologize, but I'm confused. What's the problem?"

She stared at him a second longer. But of course, she could trust her father to do one thing. And he had done it. Confirming her suspicions. Her fears. To anyone else, she supposed it might've been confusing.

But then, with a slow, dreadful sense of realization. Finding that her hands were trembling, of their own accord. She stammered, swallowed, and then whispered, "Helen is the Ghost-killer. It's Helen."

232

CHAPTER 22

Now, the three Blythes sat in the SUV with tinted windows that Tommy had procured. They were driving to the rendezvous to recover Jamie and Sophie. Her father had flat-out refused at first, but Artemis had insisted. When that hadn't worked, Tommy, who had eventually caught up with them, had threatened to punch his old man.

As much as Tommy seemed to believe their father was innocent of the crimes, he still favored his twin sister, it appeared.

But now, a strange quiet filled the cabin of the SUV.

No one had spoken for the better part of the last ten minutes.

Artemis could still feel her skin prickling. Her stomach had twisted itself like a pretzel. She couldn't believe it.

Part of her didn't want to. Part of her wanted to deny it completely.

More than once, she felt a panic attack rising. She was hyperventilating, sitting in the back seat, having allowed her father the front seat.

Her brother was driving, his fingerless gloves adhering to the leather steering wheel, his knuckles white, holding tight.

It was the only thing that made sense. *Now*, it made sense.

Night had faded, and time was quickly eating into the early morning.

It was still pitch black outside. And the dark clouds she had spotted earlier were rumbling. Storms were common in this particular area of Washington State. The winds came over the mountains, and the constant cycle of evaporation off the lakes gave way to downpours.

Already, in the distance, against the glow of lights lining the highway, she spotted sheets of water pelting the tarmac.

Miles ahead. It looked more like mist than anything. But it was the edge of the rain. They were heading toward it. Toward the gas station where they were supposed to meet the kidnapper.

It was Tommy who broke the silence first. "It can't be Helen."

This was the second time he had spoken this phrase. The first time, when she had told him, he had laughed. Now, he looked like she had kicked him in the stomach.

"It is," Artemis said quietly. "I don't understand how. But it is."

Tommy was still gripping the steering wheel tightly. He turned, glancing back.

"How can you possibly know that?" he demanded.

She said, "Because he said he didn't know who it was." She pointed at their father.

Otto was frowning. He had denied the whole thing, of course. But eventually he had drifted off into pensive silence. And now, he didn't reply. He continued to stare through the windshield, as if shell-shocked.

"Dad can be trusted to do one thing. And that's lie. He would've known who the Ghost-killer was. If Mr. Kramer could find out, so could dad!"

"So?"

Artemis was still buzzing. She glanced into the rearview mirror, catching her brother's gaze as he returned his attention to the road.

"So who's the only person he would want to protect?"

"You?"

"Besides me."

"So this confirms that Helen is alive?"

"Yes. But she's also killed seven people at least. No, sorry. Almost twelve. More, probably."

"What makes you think it's Helen?"

Suddenly, in the distance, thunder rumbled. A flash of lightning.

"All the victims were like Helen. We thought it was because Dad was targeting people like them. Because he was jealous or something. They thought he killed Helen as the culmination of his crimes."

Her father looked sick from where he was sitting in the front seat.

She continued, "The note she gave you at the waterfall. It was one of the games I won. She said Dad was innocent, said she was investigating."

"Exactly," Tommy said.

"I just. . ." Artemis trailed off.

She'd been so sure a moment ago. But something was still missing. Something didn't add up. She knew Helen. She could fetch the memories from her mind, analyzing the memories of a child with the brain of an adult; Helen had been kind. Helen had been considerate. Helen had been gentle. Helen had been everything that Artemis had wanted to be. That was still true. So how could a woman like that kill people? Helen had only been fifteen at the time. She would've had to start killing when she was young.

Her father's hands were clasped in his lap. He was gripping them tight, as if trying to squeeze the life out of his own fingers. Trying to strangle them.

"Wait, wait, wait. . ." Artemis said, her voice shaking. "If she was investigating. But she didn't. . ." Artemis trailed off. "I'm missing something. *What* am I missing?"

Tommy said, "You're missing the whole thing. Helen was not the killer. I know Helen."

Artemis shot back, "I know her too."

Tommy glanced back at her again, regarding her over the shoulder cushion. "Then we agree. It can't be Helen. It's not possible."

"But it is. All the victims looked like Helen. But there's something else. . ."

"Just stop," their father said suddenly.

"What else?"

"What if Helen was the one who framed Dad? She would've known about the camera in the bedroom. I thought it was someone who had been in our house before. But what if it really was someone who had been in our house often. What if it was Helen?"

Tommy snapped, "What if it was me? That's not proof. It's conjecture."

"I said, stop!" their father said, his voice shaking in anger.

But neither of them listened to him.

Artemis continued, "Who else would Dad be trying to protect? Who else would he be lying for?"

Tommy glared at her. He still wasn't watching the road. "In a second, I'm starting to feel like you might accuse me."

Artemis hesitated. She said, "Why would you kill those women? You were only ten. No. I don't think it was you."

Tommy shrugged once. "So why do you think it was Helen?"

"Stop!" their father repeated, more firmly.

But Artemis looked at him. And then she said, "You know what, if you're not gonna tell me what I'm missing, I know someone who will."

She pulled her phone from her pocket. *Fear.* Her father had reacted in fear when he had first heard that someone had kidnapped Jamie in order to free him from prison. Why fear?

Someone else had claimed they knew the Ghost-killer. Someone else was involved in all of it. Someone, even, who had claimed to be Helen.

And so, Artemis raised her phone. She made the call. And then they all drifted into silence as the phone began to ring, echoing faintly in the SUV. In the distance, thunder rumbled, and lightning pitchforked the sky.

The phone continued to ring.

After a second, a voice answered. "Where are you?" the voice snapped.

Artemis tensed. Her father in the front seat had gone rigid, staring through the windshield. She watched her father. Again, she hadn't been making the call to speak with the kidnapper but rather to witness her father's reaction to her speaking.

Now, she could see the way he tensed. The way he closed his eyes briefly but quickly recovered.

Tommy was staring into the rearview mirror.

"We're on our way," Artemis said firmly. "Are Jamie and Sophie there?"

"You first," said the woman on the other line. Some of her irritation faded and was now replaced by a more playful, mocking tone.

Artemis only hesitated briefly before extending the phone to her father. She watched him closely, watching every crease and line in his face.

Her father just shook his head, though, his lips sealed.

"Where is he, Artemis?" said the woman, in that same suddenly playful, singsong voice. "Time to chat, Daddy."

But Otto had gone so quiet, his face so pale, that Artemis felt shivers along her arms.

She was now motionless, sitting in the car, the phone extended. For a brief moment, she even forgot about the rendezvous. Forgot about being wanted for murder. Forgot about everything.

All she could *really* think was what her father's posture was screaming.

He lied with body language.

But Artemis could sometimes . . . just *sometimes* read through the deceptions. Now, she noticed the way his hands had folded, the fingers enclosing over the vulnerable palms. His breathing had increased. His posture had gone rigid. His head was bowed as if in some quiet grief.

Why would the voice of a woman give him grief?

Unless. . .

All of it was making sense, and yet Artemis was still missing a piece.

This woman wasn't Helen. Couldn't be. She hadn't known about the note handed to Tommy at the waterfall. She'd referred to herself in the third person, letting slip that *Helen* was someone else.

Artemis had *known* Helen growing up. This woman was as different from the kindhearted sister Artemis remembered as oil was from water.

So. . .

"I. . ." Artemis tried to speak.

And then she realized something. Something that might make sense of all of it.

She remembered something else. The comment that Fake-Helen had made over the phone. She'd known things—things she ought *not* to have known.

"No. You're thinking of our backyard camping trip. Because you think I learned this information from Dad. Or Tommy. But I'm talking

about the sister's trip. The summer weekend. Up into the mountains. Remember now?"

The words came back quickly. This kidnapper, this woman had known things she shouldn't have.

"A therapist," Artemis said suddenly, staring at the phone.

"What was that?" the voice replied.

"You . . . something you said," Artemis whispered.

She could feel Tommy watching her now, frozen. And more began to make sense. "You said. . ." Artemis trailed off. And she remembered the woman's words from before.

"My therapist," the woman had said softly, *"says I need to get control of my emotions. At least . . . she used to say that. Worthless harpy is now feeding maggots in a ditch."*

At the time, Artemis had thought it was bluster. But now. . .

"One of the victims was a therapist," Artemis whispered slowly. "You . . . you're the Ghost-killer. . ."

A pause. A silence in the vehicle.

And Artemis' mind was still spinning. This was the first time the strange woman had gone quiet on the other line. Something else was obvious now to Artemis. She'd never seen this woman's face. Not yet. The only time the two of them had ever encountered each other had

241

been at night on an old farm road, while the woman's hair had been in her eyes, her face streaked with dirt.

That had been the point when the woman had stolen Artemis' information off her phone.

But Artemis had never *seen* this woman.

"Maybe. . ." Artemis said slowly, the rising sense of horror filling her. "Maybe you should video call. You can see dad that way."

"Oh?" the voice said quietly. "He's really there, then? You're not lying to me, sister?"

Tommy was frowning deeply, listening closely.

It wasn't Helen. Her voice was wrong. Her attitude was wrong. Everything about it was wrong.

And yet . . . if *this* was the Ghost-killer.

Then this was Helen.

"I don't understand. . ." Artemis whispered, her voice shaking.

She remembered now, the Washingtons. The kidnapper had spared the Washingtons for some reason back at the ranch. Had killed Agent Butcher but had left the Washingtons alive. Strange. . .

Except not if Artemis was being told the truth.

If this *was* Helen—as impossible as that seemed—then the Washingtons were both geniuses in their own right. The Washingtons were chess masters.

Perhaps this woman had spared them out of a sense of camaraderie.

But that would only mean one thing. . .

The thing that *couldn't* be true.

"You're not Helen," Artemis whispered quietly. "You're not."

At the words, she noted the way her father flinched, then glanced back. He was frowning intensely, staring at the phone clutched in Artemis' hand.

Artemis now remembered the other things. The same things she'd been investigating recently. Break-ins had occurred in their community when Artemis had been five. That was the reason her father had installed the security camera, to protect his own home.

But the break-ins had all been in Pinelake.

Around the age when Helen had been *ten*. She'd started at ten. Then escalated. Violence could start small, at first. Could start with nonviolent behavior. Sometimes arson, sometimes burglary, sometimes other things.

Artemis was shaking horribly. Remembering it all.

Every piece now slotting into place.

243

Every piece except one.

She didn't ask this time but instead simply placed the call. Her phone swiped up, and the number began to dial.

A video call.

She just stared at the screen, watching.

The call was rejected.

She tried again, more insistently.

The voice over the speaker chuckled and said, "My-my, aren't you nosy? Mayhap there be cops with you, sister dearest?"

But Artemis just scowled, staring. "You want to see Dad? I want to see Jamie and Sophie."

But really, she wanted to see this woman.

Fake-Helen.

Fake, right?

Had to be. This wasn't her sister. She was certain of it.

But . . . but everything pointed to it *being* Helen, now.

Her father's reactions. The way he'd gone quiet, the fear in her eyes. Tommy was even staring at the phone as if he'd seen a ghost. Thunder rumbled in the distance, and droplets of rain began tapping against the vehicle as they'd reached the fringe of the tumbling rain.

The tires whirred over the water, and Tommy kept picking up speed as they raced toward their rendezvous. Tridents of bright electric blue flashed across the horizon, and Artemis could feel her heart thumping in her chest.

She wanted to scream at the phone. Wanted to throw it against the dash.

But in the end, she just placed another video call again.

Again.

Rejected. Rejected.

Another call, more insistent.

Then finally, the voice of the kidnapper, like a sibilant hiss. "We'll see each other in person, sister dearest. That's been the plan. All along. Our little family reunion. Tommy's with you, isn't he? Hmm? Yes, don't answer. I know he is. I'll see you soon, Artemis. Only family allowed, understand? Jamie hasn't been very talkative, mind. Come now. And you better hurry. No telling what I'll do when I'm upset."

She hung up.

CHAPTER 23

The video call had been left unanswered.

Why?

Again, it made no sense.

Artemis' wheels were spinning. Her father and brother were both shooting glances back at her. Tommy cursed, and the vehicle jolted as he was forced to readjust and direct his SUV back onto the road from where it had hit the safety bumps on the side.

Water sprayed. The windshield wipers whirred—*whump, whump, whump.*

Her brother and father looked as if they'd seen a ghost.

"That was Helen's voice," Tommy said sharply. "That—that was Helen!"

"No!" Artemis snapped back. "It wasn't."

"It wasn't," their father murmured under his breath.

"You're lying again!" Tommy shouted.

But Otto Blythe shook his head, and he finally turned to meet his son and daughter's gaze and hold it for longer than a split second.

His eyes held grief there.

And . . . and something Artemis was *not* accustomed to seeing.

Tears.

His blue, cold eyes brimmed with tears. His voice shook as he said, "Your sister. . ." he swallowed. "She was my favorite."

He just let the words linger there, allowing them access to this revelation.

It didn't cut. How could it? Artemis had considered herself dead to this man for decades.

"She . . . she was my oldest," he said. "She looked the most like your mother." Otto's voice was shaking now. "Things . . . things were good for years. When she was on her medication."

"What?" Artemis said, frowning. "I never saw Helen take anything."

"She . . . she stopped. She shouldn't have. She was embarrassed by it. She never let you see," Otto was murmuring.

"I don't get it," Artemis whispered.

"I do," Tommy said suddenly, staring. "I saw her take those pills. I used to. . ." he trailed off, wincing. He grimaced, then muttered, "I told some guys it was ecstasy and sold it to them." Tommy quickly added, "But only a few pills. I found them under her bed."

Their father was staring down again, his head bowed once more like a man in mourning.

"I don't understand!" Artemis said, and she was growing frustrated with how frequently she seemed to be uttering this phrase.

Before her father could reply, though.

There was a sudden ringing sound.

Brring.

Brrrrrring.

Artemis glanced down.

Her phone on her lap. A video call coming in. They all stared at the device, all of them motionless and quiet.

Artemis took the phone, answering it. Her fingers were shaking.

Then, a face appeared. A familiar face, in some ways. But older now. Still, the memories returned. The face was clear, the hair brushed to the side.

And Artemis nearly dropped the phone as if it were scalding.

Helen had always been the more beautiful of the two. Helen had curly hair, where Artemis' was straight and black. Helen had been taller than Artemis, and she didn't have mismatched eyes, which everyone seemed to notice whenever Artemis entered the room. Helen's eyes had been gentle lavender, like the flower. Helen had Bambi eyes, sharper cheekbones, and an upturned, celestial nose that had always made Artemis jealous.

Helen had also been the smarter of the two.

Artemis had known this. She'd been five years younger at the time.

Now, though . . . she found herself staring into those familiar lavender eyes. Found her gaze tracing those familiar bronze curls.

The woman on the video looked as if she was in pain. Sweat was prickling down her forehead. Her teeth were set tightly together. She shook and murmured, "Artemis. . . Artemis, please. Turn around. She wants to kill you. Don't come here! Leave!"

It looked as if each word cost Helen.

As if each word pained Artemis' older sister.

But all Artemis could do was stare at the phone. Frozen. Her father's words, Tommy's corroboration. Medication?

And now the final piece slotted into place.

Helen was *not* the Ghost-killer.

But Helen *was* the Ghost-killer.

Helen was *not* the kidnapper.

But Helen *was* the kidnapper.

The number she'd called from was the same number as the woman who Artemis had called Fake-Helen.

"Helen?" Artemis whispered, her voice shaking. "Helen, is it really you?"

Tears brimmed in Helen's eyes as she stared through the screen. The beautiful woman nodded once. She would have been thirty-five this past September. She was still gritting her teeth, though, and one hand was massaging her forehead.

Helen whispered. "P-please, don't come. She wants to kill you. To kill Dad! Don't come!"

"Who?" Artemis demanded. "Helen! Helen, please—we can help you!"

And as she spoke, and as she felt the weight of the witnesses in the car, staring in horror at the phone, the scene transformed.

It was like watching a snake shed its skin. One moment, Helen had been massaging her forehead, gritting her teeth as if struggling with immense willpower against something.

The next, it was as if the face itself morphed.

Instead of tense and in pain, the face was relaxed. The eyes didn't carry tears—which were flicked away with a callous finger—but rather twinkled with amusement.

The same lips which had been pressed into a thin line now relaxed as well and curled into a knowing, teasing smile.

"Oh my, Artemis," said this woman. "The cat's out of the bag, isn't it? Tut-tut. Helen has been *so* scared of you finding out for so long. She's going to be downright embarrassed!" The thought seemed to please this woman.

A woman wearing the same face, the same features.

But a different person.

At least. . . A different personality.

Multiple personality disorder? Artemis didn't know the clinical terms. But she stared into the phone, frozen in place.

Now it made sense.

Helen had given the note to Tommy at the waterfall . . . while she'd been in control. If that was how it worked. But this woman . . . this strange inhabitant—this . . . *Ghost-killer* hadn't known about the note.

Helen had been investigating. . .

Herself. Had she not known?

Artemis just stared, her heart momentarily feeling as if it had stopped in her chest. Her eyes were wide, round like saucers.

She stared at the screen . . . at the smiling face.

And then she heard the sound of raindrops. A flash of lightning on the screen—the rumble of thunder.

She peered closer, frowning, and realized that the woman in the video was driving a vehicle. She could see the seatbelt, the cushioned chair.

"You know," said the woman casually. "I . . . I hate to say this, but I haven't been entirely honest with you, Artemis."

"What . . . what's. . ." Artemis couldn't even finish the sentence.

"Trust me. Helen has been *trying* to control it. She really has, you'd be proud of her. Of me. Of us." A flash of a smile. "But after so long . . . you know how it is. Helen didn't even know what we were doing. She thought she was sleeping." A chuckle. "But don't you see, *Artemis*? It's all a game. It's always been a game. And I won."

Artemis stammered, "You . . . let's talk. Okay? We can talk about this." She wasn't even sure *what* she was saying. If anything, Artemis felt as if she was simply buying time.

She heard the thunder rumble again, at the same time as it did on the phone.

She spotted motion through the windshield, ahead.

Headlights. Bright, beaming headlights, coming toward them.

On the *same* side of the road.

"There's only one route from Pinelake to that station," Helen said conversationally. She smiled. "I apologize. . . But I'm not here to exchange anyone. Goodbye, Artemis. It's been a fun game."

And then the woman hung up.

Artemis stared through the windshield. The oncoming truck was picking up speed, faster—faster, like some great shark tearing through a breaker wave.

It kept coming toward them. The brights were turned on, attempting to blind them.

"Shit. . ." Tommy was muttering. "What the hell does this guy think he's—"

"It's her!" Artemis said suddenly, horror welling up. "Go off the road!" She screamed, "TOMMY, GET OFF THE ROAD!"

Her brother reacted a split second too late.

He began to veer.

But the giant oncoming truck barreled toward them. The lights flashing now, almost in the same rhythm as the woman's taunting chuckles had come over the phone.

Artemis screamed.

Her brother shouted as he veered sharply. Their father cursed, gripping the dash in front of him.

And then, on the dark, rain-dappled night road, the collision.

CHAPTER 24

Shattered glass had scattered everywhere. Artemis groaned faintly. Her head was pounding. She felt a trickle of warmth down the side of her face and realized her hair was hanging to the side. . . The car was toppled. She spotted the asphalt to her left, suggesting the car had landed on its left doors.

Now, she felt water drizzling through the shattered passenger windows, coming down and tapping against her skin, helping to rouse her.

Lightning flashed again.

Her heart pounded. Her father was lying unconscious in front of her. His head lolled to the side. Her brother was groaning as well, trying to recover. His fingers, bloodied and flecked with glass which clung to the blood, were tearing at the seatbelt, trying to extricate it.

In her brother's other hand, she spotted him groping at his glove compartment. A gun. He was withdrawing a gun.

But the weapon clattered, fell. And it nearly struck Artemis on the cheek as it toppled into the plastic pocket in the door at her side.

Everything was upside down. The only thing keeping her from falling to the base was the seatbelt strap.

She groaned again.

More thunder. And then. . .

The sound of a revving engine.

Her phone was ringing somewhere, but she couldn't see it. Her head continued to spin. And then. . .

It all came flooding back.

Helen was the Ghost-killer.

Helen had a secondary personality that had taken control. Helen had been investigating the crimes herself . . . likely having been suspicious of what was happening.

Helen had framed their father for the murders.

Helen had been targeting women she'd been jealous of. It was all a game—that was what she'd said.

And now Artemis was the newest opponent.

The newest threat.

The woman was trying to kill Helen's family.

She could hear the rumbling of an engine. Glimpsed, in the mirror, the large truck pulling back from the crash, wheels whirring. The blazing headlights continued to glare, to illuminate the ground.

The vehicle picked up speed again.

Artemis cursed, bracing once more.

The truck skidded as it approached, slowing only briefly.

This, Artemis guessed, was all that stopped them from being crushed. Still . . . the collision came a second time.

Her body jolted. Pain flared.

The sound of crunching metal filled the air as the car flipped, rolling once, twice, three times as it plummeted off the side of the road. Stars danced before her eyes as the violent motion sent her careening from side to side, her body pressed into the hard, cold surface of the back seat.

The car had come to a shuddering, crashing halt, and she found herself upside down, her head pressed against the ceiling and her feet dangling above her. There was a tense moment of silence before the screams began, desperate and panicked. She let out a gasp, her breath coming in short, shallow bursts as she attempted to catch her breath. She was panting, her heart thumping as her mind raced to find a way out.

But then, she heard it again. A third time. Helen wasn't going to stop until her family was dead. The sound of an engine, growing louder and louder as it approached. Fear coursed through her veins as the realization of what was happening hit her like a freight train. The truck dipped over the edge of the incline, like some child peeking into its parents' room. And then it came barreling toward them. There was no time to think, no time to act. She had to get out of the car before it was too late.

Desperate, she clawed at the door, trying to pry it open. It refused to budge, and her heart sank as she realized that she was trapped. Then, she heard the sound of the truck's engine grow louder, and she knew that she had only seconds to escape. Taking a deep breath, she braced herself against the seat and kicked the door with all her strength.

The truck had to dip now, over the incline as it came for them.

Where was Jamie?

Where was Sophie?

None of it could be answered.

Not yet.

She had to escape. Had to stop the truck. Her brother was still moving. Her father still unconscious, but if Artemis didn't do something, they'd all die.

Now, the large truck had hit them again but this time was shoving them. Moving them toward the edge of a steep incline off the side of the road.

As they scraped along the ground, gouging earth and furrowing mud, Artemis kicked again. She felt the door give way. Last second, something tapped against her arm.

The cold metal of the gun Tommy had dropped. She snatched it, hyperventilating, and then she scrambled out of the car, her clothing snagging on the jagged metal as she clambered out onto the road. She aimed. Fired twice.

The truck's front tires exploded as it prepared to ram again.

Artemis heard the sound of honking and raised her gun.

Firing once more.

She couldn't bring herself to shoot at the cabin. Couldn't aim toward Helen.

How could she?

It was still her sister.

Helen was trapped. Taken captive by her own mind. Such a brilliant . . . but so very, very *powerful* mind.

Instead, Artemis had aimed for the next tire. It burst as well. Now, panting and trembling, her body shaking with adrenaline, Artemis stumbled forward. The truck had gone still. Tires flat and whirring uselessly in the mud it had churned.

There was a moment of complete stillness before she was finally able to gather her bearings.

The SUV was upside down, its windows shattered and its doors twisted and broken. The truck was motionless.

And a figure's silhouette was visible in the dark.

Artemis aimed her weapon toward the cabin, her hand trembling. Her voice shook as well, as she called out. "Get out of the cab, Helen! Get out!" she demanded.

But nothing happened.

The figure didn't move.

Artemis stumbled forward, reaching for the cab door with shaking fingers. Then it flung open. The truck door slammed her in the chest, sending her stumbling back.

A figure followed, like a bat surging from hell.

A woman wearing a raincoat. Her bronze curls quickly drenched under the rain as she hopped into the mud.

Artemis pushed off the ground, slowly regaining her feet, gun tight in her grip as she faced her long-lost sister.

Helen and Artemis stared at each other, both of them still, frozen in place.

Artemis then heard shouting. Desperate yelling. "Artemis!" Jamie's voice was calling. "Artemis, are you okay!"

She could hear crying too. The sounds of Sophie.

Artemis' heart jolted in her chest.

But she didn't cry out. She couldn't. She didn't have the energy to even speak. Now, she just stared at where her older sister was framed in the open truck door. Her sister's shoes pressed into the mud. The woman was glaring at Artemis, shaking her head side to side.

"You really are a nuisance, aren't you?" snapped the woman, raising her voice to be heard over the thunder.

"Helen," Artemis said cautiously, gun still in hand. "Helen, please. It's *me*. Please!"

But Helen's eyes narrowed. She looked at the gun in her sister's hand. And Artemis spotted something flash in Helen's. Not a knife. A cable.

Black cable, like electrical wire.

Artemis felt her stomach in her throat.

"Helen! Please!" Artemis cried. "Don't make me shoot you!" Terror and grief and awe and horror all swirled through her. She wasn't sure *what* to do. She didn't know what she *could* do.

"You know, I was telling you the truth at times," said Helen quietly. "I do have the evidence to *prove* you didn't kill Azin. Or Butcher. I have it right here." She pulled her phone from her pocket, wiggling it.

Then she smirked and tossed the phone into the truck behind her.

She took a strong stance, feet at shoulder width, arms crossed, electrical cord clutched in one hand. There was a taunting look in her gaze.

"All you have to do," she murmured, "to clear your name, to clear Dad's name, even, to help Jamie, Sophie. . . Put a bullet in me."

She grinned widely, like a jack-o'-lantern. "That's all, Artemis. Just kill Helen. Can you do it?"

She didn't show an ounce of fear. Didn't flinch but stood there, facing her younger sister, staring as if in some taunt.

Artemis was facing the Ghost-killer. This wasn't Helen. Helen was imprisoned somewhere. Artemis didn't even speak to the Ghost-killer. Instead, her voice shaking, she whispered, "Helen, *please*. I'm here to help you! I'm here to help!"

"Oh, stop that. I've been in the driver's seat for quite some time, Artemis. Helen put up a fight," said the woman conversationally, "but her mistake . . . do you want to know what it was?"

Artemis was still clutching the gun, which was now slick with rain.

"I'll tell you," Helen murmured. "Her mistake was leaving you. I didn't realize it at the time. But the more isolated she was . . . the stronger I grew. She *needed* me to protect her. She was too weak for the world." A chuckle. The woman shook her head, and droplets of rain trickled down her beautiful features.

Artemis let out a shuddering breath. She could hear Jamie calling out. She spotted the phone, which apparently had the evidence to clear her name.

She tensed, swallowed once. . .

It would have been so simple to raise the weapon. Fire twice. End it all.

But of course. . . There wasn't a chance in hell that Artemis would shoot her own sister.

"I'm trying to help," Artemis said firmly. "Please, Helen. *Please.* Tell me you're there."

A pause, a brief flicker. The woman looked temporarily confused. But then, her mask returned. In that moment, however, in that glimmer, Artemis spotted hope. Something in her sister's eyes. Something she recognized.

But it was gone just as quickly.

And then, Helen screamed and flung herself at Artemis. Indifferent to the gun or—perhaps—hoping Artemis would *use* it.

CHAPTER 25

Artemis couldn't bring herself to shoot, so she flung the weapon clear.

The taller woman collided with her sister. The two of them hit the ground, hard. Pain flared through Artemis' back. The mud slicked her. She tried to scramble to her feet, both of them grappling for control.

The rain poured down from the night sky in thick sheets, obscuring the sight of the two women as they fought for their lives, embraced in a violent struggle.

The two combatants had been adversaries of a *different* variety for some time. Chess was a game of the mind, but this was the first time they had come to blows. Helen had taken Artemis by surprise, wrapping a length of electrical cord around her neck in that first lunge, with the practiced motions of the Ghost-killer's favorite weapon. Now, Helen was trying to squeeze the life out of Artemis. The air was heavy, thick with the smell of asphalt and wetness as the fierce rain pelted against the highway and the two women.

Artemis was determined, but Helen had the advantage of leverage, her feet planted firmly on the ground as she leaned in, using her weight to press the cord tighter and tighter around Artemis' neck.

Artemis fought back with everything she had, pushing desperately against her attacker, her hands clawing at the cord, trying to pry it away from her neck. She kicked back with her legs and twisted her body, trying to break away from the grip that Helen had clamped around her. But Helen was relentless, her grip only tightening as she pressed her advantage.

Artemis managed to break free for a moment and spun around to face her attacker, her breath coming in ragged gasps. They both stared at each other in the rain, determination in their eyes. Hatred flared in Helen's . . . but also confusion.

"Artemis?" whispered a voice. A much softer, gentler voice. A whimper of a voice. But then the scowl returned.

This time, as if prompted by that faint mewl for help, Artemis moved first, lunging forward and grabbing Helen by the wrists. She clamped down hard, preventing Helen from using the cord again, and the two of them grappled with each other in the wetness.

Helen managed to break and twist away from Artemis, but Artemis was quick on her feet and managed to catch up with her. She grabbed Helen by the collar and yanked her back, pummeling her with wild punches, trying to make her release the cord. Artemis wasn't the *punching* sort. She felt entirely out of her element.

But everything about this had stretched her to capacity. Terror and horror filled her.

In the chaos of the fight, Artemis managed to push Helen away and stumbled backward, her back pressed against the cold metal of a guardrail. She looked up to see Helen advancing toward her, the cord held tightly in her hands. Without thinking, Artemis grabbed the guardrail and used it to launch herself at Helen, her body connecting with her attacker and sending them both tumbling to the ground.

Artemis scrambled to her feet and tried to make a break for it, but Helen was already up and had a firm grip on the cord again. In desperation, Artemis managed to grab hold of Helen's arm, and the two of them wrestled in the rain, struggling for control of the cord.

Finally, Artemis managed to break free, but Helen was still standing between her and the road. She eyed her attacker warily, her body tense and ready to fight.

Helen gave her a wicked grin and launched herself at Artemis, the cord held tightly in her hands. But this time, Artemis was ready. She ducked and weaved, dodging the cord and Helen's punches. Then, in one swift motion, she grabbed Helen's arm and twisted it behind her, wrenching the cord from her grip.

Helen gasped in pain and stumbled away, her face a mask of hatred and defeat. Artemis stood motionless, the cord in her hands, her body shaking with exertion.

The rain continued to pour down around them, but neither of them moved. Artemis stared at Helen for a long moment, her eyes hard and determined.

And then she spotted the item in Helen's hand.

The gun.

She'd recovered the gun. She raised it slowly, pointing it at Artemis.

Artemis had the cord but went still, staring wide-eyed at the gun. She didn't react. Didn't know *how* to react or what even to say. Instead, she stood motionless, frozen in place.

The gun was pointed at her head.

Artemis let out a trembling breath. She swallowed.

Helen kept the gun raised; her finger tightened.

But she didn't fire.

"Helen. . ." Artemis whispered, her voice coming in gasps. Her body bruised, drenched. Her form motionless. "Helen, please. . . It's *me.*"

Hatred flashed in those eyes. But still, the finger remained tensed.

"Come on. . ." Helen was whispering. "Just do it! DO IT, YOU STUPID BITCH!"

But the gun didn't fire. Couldn't.

Then the same voice from earlier. An exhausted, weary, desperate voice. "Please. . . Artemis. . . *Run!*"

But Artemis didn't. She stared her sister directly in the eyes. How many years had she wondered about Helen? How many years had she hoped, desperately?

No. . .

No, she wasn't going to run. Wasn't going to leave Helen trapped. Kidnapped just like Jamie. A different type of ensnaring, but still a captivity.

"No," Artemis said simply, shaking her head.

The gentler voice was crying again. "Please!" it pleaded. "Artemis—I can't stop her. Run!"

"NO!" Artemis yelled back, dripping mud, dripping rainwater.

Helen's eyes flared in panic. And then she gasped, as if trying to hold on for dear life. "Please. . ." she moaned again.

"No!"

Helen was panicked now. As if realizing something, her eyes widened. She turned the gun toward her own head, pressing it against her temple.

"I'm so sorry, Art," whispered the gentle voice.

The finger began to squeeze.

Artemis screamed, surging forward. "No!" she cried. But too late. Too far. She wasn't going to stop in time.

The trigger squeezed. Helen was taking her own life while she had control. Saving her sister.

And then.

Whack!

Not a gunshot.

A blow.

The gun never went off.

One moment, Helen had been standing there, desperate, gun to her head. The next, a figure—who Artemis hadn't spotted sneaking up from behind—struck Helen on the back of the head.

Jamie Kramer stood there, gripping a piece of broken metal that had twisted off the front of the truck.

Jamie was breathing heavily. A handcuff dangled limply from his wrist. The other hand, the free hand, was mangled. The thumb looked broken. As if Jamie had broken it to free himself.

He was breathing raggedly, staring down at the woman who was lying unconscious in the mud at his feet.

He called out, "Sophie, stay in the truck! We're safe! Stay there!"

269

And then, he dropped the broken metal club.

Artemis stared at Jamie Kramer.

He stared back.

Both of them were soaked. She more so than him, and she was also streaked with mud.

They were both trembling. Artemis felt tears mingling with the rain. She glanced down at her sister, frozen in place. And then she collapsed to her knees.

It was all just too much.

She knelt there, weeping in the mud, facing Helen. "Please . . . please. . ." she kept whispering. She wasn't even sure what she was pleading.

In a way. . .

It almost felt as if her family was back.

She shot a quick look toward the SUV, her eyes still stinging with tears. Jamie was helping Otto out of the car. Both were breathing, both bruised but very much alive.

Her father wasn't a killer.

Helen was alive.

Tommy was with them.

Jamie. . . Jamie had made it.

She wasn't used to happy endings. She didn't know if this qualified. Helen was in a horrible bondage. Helen wasn't alright.

But . . . but what was it that the woman had said? The mistake Helen had made was *leaving* her family. Isolating herself.

She had killed people.

Many of them.

Artemis was wanted by the cops. Her father too. She shot a look toward the phone in the truck. Evidence to clear her name.

Her shoulders shook as she sobbed.

She felt a hand rest on her and glanced up. Jamie stooped next to her, breathing in shallow puffs, gingerly resting his injured, broken hand. But his other hand cradled her head. He kissed her on the forehead where she knelt in the mud.

"We really," he whispered, "need to stop meeting in the rain." His teeth chattered from the cold.

She wanted to laugh, but all she could do was cry and shake. She hadn't been one for crying before. Hadn't really learned how to let it out. Ever since Helen had vanished.

But now Helen was back.

It was far, far worse than she'd imagined.

But Helen was alive.

"I have to help her," Artemis whispered.

Jamie murmured, "What?"

He didn't know who Helen was. Didn't know any of it. And so, she said nothing but just remained kneeling, crying. Jamie held her tight. She could hear her brother approaching. Her father too.

"We need to get out of here, Art!" Tommy was calling. "Before cops show up. We need to get Helen somewhere safe!"

She shot her brother a look, peering under Jamie's wet sleeve, which wrapped around her in an embrace.

Her brother was already hastening toward them. He began to lift Helen.

Jamie frowned, beginning to protest.

But Artemis said, "It's my sister, Jamie. She's not well. She's sick."

Jamie just stared. He went rigid, stepping back, staring at her. Sophie was crying again from the back seat. He glanced distractedly toward the truck. He pointed at the woman on the ground. "She's evil, Artemis. Insane."

Artemis shook her head. Helen had just saved Artemis' life. Had stopped the woman from shooting her. Had been willing to shoot herself to save Artemis.

"No," Artemis said firmly. "No, she's not!"

Artemis had been right. The woman on the phone was *not* Helen. It was Helen's captor.

"She's not!" Artemis insisted, louder.

She struggled to her feet, stooping to help Tommy lift Helen. Their father opened the truck door again, gesturing at them. The family moved quickly, Helen's body limp. Jamie just watched, looking stunned, scared.

His sister was still crying, though. So he turned, hastening back toward the rear of the vehicle.

Artemis' arms strained as she lifted her sister, with Tommy and their father guiding Helen into the front passenger seat of the truck.

"Tires are flat!" Artemis warned with a shout.

But Tommy shook his head. "It'll get us out of here. It's fine. Shit—my gun." He hopped from the cabin, snatched the weapon from the ground, then returned.

"The SUV?" Otto murmured in his son's ear from where the eldest Blythe was now crowding in the front seat. Artemis sat between the two seats. The four of them pressed tightly together like sardines while Tommy was at the driver's seat.

Artemis hesitated, then said, "I should check on Jamie."

Tommy shrugged. "Fine. Just tell him to hang on tight. We need to get going. Now!"

She nodded quickly, pushing out of the front seat. As she did, she snatched the phone that Helen had indicated, slipping it into her pocket. The phone that would clear her name, supposedly.

She paused as she lowered from the truck, her hand gripping a cold metal handle.

They couldn't turn Helen in. Artemis wouldn't do it. She refused.

They'd have to be smart. Clever. Figure out a way to bring Helen back, to help her.

Artemis stared at her sister's unconscious face. She looked so . . . peaceful like that. Artemis swallowed back a sob as her brother shouted, "Come on, Art! Hurry up!"

She nodded quickly, slipping from the cabin and back into the mud to move around the back of the truck and speak to Jamie.

He was alive. Sophie was alive.

Helen was alive.

Artemis paused only briefly. She couldn't turn Helen in. . . She *couldn't*.

She nodded as she rounded the truck, making a promise to herself. An oath.

No matter what . . . she'd expend her own life to make sure Helen could be free again. The Helen Artemis knew. The one she'd always known. Helen was still in there. She'd glimpsed it.

Helen was alive.

And in a way . . . the game had only really just begun.

It was now up to Artemis, she decided, to outwit this imposter. To outplay this kidnapper. To recover her sister.

To recover the one thing she'd always wanted but never had.

A family.

The game had *truly* just begun.

What's Next for Artemis

She Slips Away

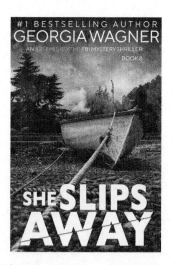

Artemis has her life back, but she needs to lay low for a while. She retreats to a sleepy beachside resort for some much needed R&R.

But then two teenagers go missing. According to security, though, they never left their rooms. Now, Artemis is reluctantly dragged back into a game of cat and mouse in an old castle-turned-hotel. Amidst the ancient, imported stone work, and the luxurious resort amenities, she hunts a killer who strikes without a trace.

At the same time, she's still in contact with her family of fugitives. She knows it isn't advised, but Artemis considers bringing in her own father to help on this most baffling case.

Also by Georgia Wagner

Girl Under the Ice

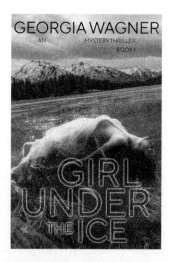

Once a rising star in the FBI, with the best case closure rate of any investigator, Ella Porter is now exiled to a small gold mining town bordering the wilderness of Alaska. The reason for her

new assignment? She allowed a prolific serial killer to escape custody.

But what no one knows is that she did it on purpose.

The day she shows up in Nome, bags still unpacked, the wife of the richest gold miner in town goes missing. This is the second woman to vanish in as many days. And it's up to Ella to find out what happened.

Assigning Ella to Nome is no accident, either. Though she swore she'd never return, Ella grew up in the small, gold mining town, treated like royalty as a child due to her own family's wealth. But like all gold tycoons, the Porter family secrets are as dark as Ella's own.

WANT TO KNOW MORE?

Greenfield press is the brainchild of bestselling author Steve Higgs. He specializes in writing fast paced adventurous mystery and urban fantasy with a humorous lilt. Having made his money publishing his own work, Steve went looking for a few 'special' authors whose work he believed in.

Georgia Wagner was the first of those, but to find out more and to be the first to hear about new releases and what is coming next, you can join the Facebook group by copying the following link into your browser - www.facebook.com/GreenfieldPress.

ABOUT THE AUTHOR

Georgia Wagner worked as a ghost writer for many, many years before finally taking the plunge into self-publishing. Location and character are two big factors for Georgia, and getting those right allows the story to flow seamlessly onto the page. And flow it does, because Georgia is so prolific a new term is required to describe the rate at which nerve-tingling stories find their way into print.

When not found attached to a laptop, Georgia likes spending time in local arboretums, among the trees and ponds. An avid cultivator of orchids, begonias, and all things floral, Georgia also has a strong penchant for art, paintings, and sculptures. A many-decades long passion for mystery novels and years of chess tournament experience makes Georgia the perfect person to pen the Artemis Blythe series.

Printed in Great Britain
by Amazon

43237051R00159